WEATHER

WEATHER

JENNY OFFILL

THORNDIKE PRESS
A part of Gale, a Cengage Company

Copyright © 2020 by Jenny Offill.
Thorndike Press, a part of Gale, a Cengage Company.

Thorndike Press® Large Print Basic.
The text of this Large Print edition is unabridged.
Other aspects of the book may vary from the original edition.
Set in 16 pt. Plantin.

LIBRARY OF CONGRESS CIP DATA ON FILE.
CATALOGUING IN PUBLICATION FOR THIS BOOK
IS AVAILABLE FROM THE LIBRARY OF CONGRESS

ISBN-13: 978-1-4328-7772-9 (hardcover alk. paper)

Published in 2020 by arrangement with Alfred A. Knopf, an imprint of
The Knopf Doubleday Publishing Group, a division of Penguin Random
House, LLC

Printed in Mexico
Print Number: 01   Print Year: 2020

FOR LYDIA

NOTES FROM A TOWN MEETING IN MILFORD, CONNECTICUT, 1640:

Voted, that the earth is the Lord's and the fullness thereof; voted, that the earth is given to the Saints; voted, that we are the Saints.

ONE

ONE

In the morning, the one who is mostly enlightened comes in. There are stages and she is in the second to last, she thinks. This stage can be described only by a Japanese word. "Bucket of black paint," it means.

I spend some time pulling books for the doomed adjunct. He has been working on his dissertation for eleven years. I give him reams of copy paper. Binder clips and pens. He is writing about a philosopher I have never heard of. He is minor, but instrumental, he told me. Minor but instrumental!

But last night, his wife put a piece of paper on the fridge. *Is what you're doing right now making money?* it said.

The man in the shabby suit does not want his fines lowered. He is pleased to contribute to our institution. The blond girl whose nails are bitten to the quick stops by after lunch and leaves with a purse full of toilet paper.

I brave a theory about vaccinations and another about late capitalism. "Do you ever wish you were thirty again?" asks the lonely heart engineer. "No, never," I say. I tell him that old joke about going backward.

We don't serve time travelers here.
A time traveler walks into the bar.

On the way home, I pass the lady who sells whirling things. Sometimes when the students are really stoned, they'll buy them. "No takers today," she says. I pick out one for Eli. It's blue and white, but blurs to blue in the wind. Don't forget quarters, I remember.

At the bodega, Mohan gives me a roll of them. I admire his new cat, but he tells me

12

it just wandered in. He will keep it though because his wife no longer loves him.

"I wish you were a real shrink," my husband says. "Then we'd be rich."

■ ■ ■ ■

Henry's late. And this after I took a car service so I wouldn't be. When I finally spot him, he's drenched. No coat, no umbrella. He stops at the corner, gives change to the woman in the trashbag poncho.

My brother told me once that he missed drugs because they made the world stop calling to him. Fair enough, I said. We were at the supermarket. All around us things tried to announce their true nature. But their radiance was faint and fainter still beneath the terrible music.

I try to get him warmed up quickly: soup, coffee. He looks good, I think. Clear-eyed. The waitress makes a new pot, flirts with him. People used to stop my mother on the street. What a waste, they'd say. Eyelashes like that on a boy!

So now we have extra bread. I eat three pieces while my brother tells me a story about his NA meeting. A woman stood up and started ranting about antidepressants. What upset her most was that people were not disposing of them properly. They tested worms in the city sewers and found they contained high concentrations of Paxil and Prozac.

When birds ate these worms, they stayed closer to home, made more elaborate nests, but appeared unmotivated to mate. "But were they happier?" I ask him. "Did they get more done in a given day?"

■ ■ ■ ■

The window in our bedroom is open. You can see the moon if you lean out and crane your neck. The Greeks thought it was the only heavenly object similar to Earth. Plants and animals fifteen times stronger than our own inhabited it.

My son comes in to show me something. It looks like a pack of gum, but it's really a trick. When you try to take a piece, a metal spring snaps down on your finger. "It hurts more than you think," he warns me.

Ow.

I tell him to look out the window. "That's a waxing crescent," Eli says. He knows as much now about the moon as he ever will, I suspect. At his old school, they taught him a song to remember all its phases. Sometimes he'll sing it for us at dinner, but only if we do not request it.

The moon will be fine, I think. No one's worrying about the moon.

■ ■ ■ ■

The woman with the bullhorn is at the school door this morning. She's warning the parents not to go in, to leave the children there behind the red line. "Safety first!" she yells. "Safety first!"

But sometimes Eli cries if he's left in that loud scrum of people. He doesn't like having to walk alone from one side of that huge cafeteria to the other. Once he froze in the middle until some aide grabbed him by the elbow and pushed him toward his corner.

So today we make a run for it and dart past her to his assigned assembly point. His friend is at the table and has animal crackers, so I make it out of there without tears, but not before the bullhorn woman screams at me. "No parents! No parents may accompany their children!"

God, she loves that bullhorn. Something shoots through my body at the sound of her voice, then I'm out on the street again, telling myself not to think.

I'm not allowed to think about how big this school is or how small he is. I've made that mistake after other drop-offs. I should be used to it by now, but sometimes I get spooked all over again.

■ ■ ■ ■

All day long cranky professors. I swear the ones with tenure are the crankiest. They will cut past other people in line to check out a book or set up their hold list. Studies have shown that 94% of college professors think that they do above average work.

They gave us a guide the other day. *Tips for Dealing with Problem Patrons.* The professors weren't mentioned. There were the following categories.

Malodorous
Humming
Laughing
Defacing
Laundering
Combative
Chattering
Lonely
Coughing

But how to categorize this elderly gentleman who keeps asking me to give him the password for his own email? I try to explain that it is not possible for me to know this, that only he knows this, but he just shakes his head in that indignant way that means, What kind of help desk is this?

■ ■ ■ ■

There's a poster of Sylvia at the bus stop. It says she's coming to give a talk on campus. Years ago, I was her grad student, but then I gave up on it. She used to check in on me sometimes to see if I was still squandering my promise. The answer was always yes. Finally, she pulled some strings to get me this job even though I don't have a proper degree for it.

On the way home, I listen to her new podcast. This episode is called "The Center Cannot Hold." They could all be called that. But Sylvia's voice is almost worth the uptick in dread. It's soothing to me even though

she talks only of the invisible horsemen gal-
loping toward us.

There are recognizable patterns of ascent
and decline. But our industrial civilization
is so vast, it has such reach . . .

I look out the window. Something in the
distance, limping toward the trees.

■ ■ ■ ■

The door opens and Eli hurls himself at me.
I help him peel some rubber cement off his
hands, then he goes back to his game. This
is the one that everyone likes. It is a 3-D
procedurally generated world, according to
my husband. Educational.

It's fun to watch them play. They put
together buildings block by block, then fill
the rooms with minerals that they have
mined with pickaxes they have made. They
assemble green fields and raise chickens to

eat. "I killed one!" Eli yells. "It's almost night," Ben tells him.

There are bills and supermarket flyers. Also a magazine addressed to a former tenant. The cover promises tips for helping depressive people.

What *to* say:

> I'm sorry that you're in so much pain. I am not going to leave you. I am going to take care of myself, so you don't need to worry that your pain might hurt me.

What *not* to say:

> Have you tried chamomile tea?

■ ■ ■ ■

I let my brother choose the movie for once, but then it's so stupid I can barely watch it.

In the movies he likes there is always some great disaster about to happen and only one unlikely person who can stop it.

Afterward, we walk in the park. He's met someone maybe. But he doesn't think it's going to work out. She's too different from him. It takes me a while to figure out they haven't even been on a date yet. "You don't want to date someone like you, do you?" I ask him. Henry laughs. "God, no."

In the first class I ever took with Sylvia, she told us about assortative mating. Meaning like with like — depressive with depressive. The problem with assortative mating, she said, is that it feels perfectly correct when you do it. Like a key fitting into a lock and opening a door. The question being: Is this really the room you want to spend your life in?

So I tell my brother how Ben and I never notice the same things. Like that time I came home and he was all excited because they finally took it down. Took what down? I asked. And he had to explain that the scaffolding that had covered the front of our building for three years was finally gone. And then last week, when I was telling him a story about the guy from 5C, he said, Wait, what drug dealer?

■ ■ ■ ■

When I get home, the dog wants an ice cube. I give her one, but she keeps banging her bowl around the kitchen. "How was your day?" I ask Ben. He shrugs. "I coded mostly, did some laundry."

There is a heroic tower of folded things on the table. I spot my favorite shirt, my least depressing underwear. I go into the bedroom and change into them. Now I am a brand-new person.

On her third day of marriage, Queen Victoria wrote: *My dearest Albert put on my stockings for me. I went and saw him shave, a great delight . . .*

My mother calls and speaks to me of the light, the vine, the living bread.

■ ■ ■ ■

Seven a.m. and Eli is playing fetch. I take the slobber frog away, put it on top of the fridge. "We have to go! Get your backpack!" I tell him. The dog watches me warily, her head on her paws. I run a brush roughly through Eli's hair. He winces and darts away from me. "We have to go! Put on your shoes!" I yell. Then finally, we're out the door.

Mrs. Kovinski tries to tell me something about the elevators, but we race right past her. Ten blocks. I'm walking too fast, pulling Eli along with me. Wrong living, I know, I know, but it's a long line at the office if he's late.

A last sprint across the playground and we make it just in time. I'm out of breath, sweaty, sad. I kiss Eli's head, trying to undo

23

the rush. Why didn't I have more kids so I could have more chances?

These other mothers knew enough not to have only one. There is a cluster of them over by the fence. They are speaking Urdu, I think. One of them smiles at me and I give a little wave.

How do I look to her? I wonder, in my drab clothes and fancy glasses. Last week, she donated a bag of silk fabric for the school raffle; it is red, stitched through with golden thread. Eli wants to win it and use it for a cape. I know how to write her name, but not how to say it.

■ ■ ■ ■

This woman is a shrink. Also a Buddhist. She likes to practice one or the other on me, I've noticed. "You seem to identify down, not up. Why do you think that is?"

You tell me, lady.

24

On Tuesdays, she teaches a meditation class in the basement. It is open to the whole community, not just university people. I've noticed that Margot listens differently than I do. She pays attention, but leaves her own stories out of it.

It's slow today so I help her set up for class. Cushions for the strong, chairs for the weak. "You should stay," she always tells me, but I never do. Not sure where to sit.

■ ■ ■ ■

Here is the midnight question for my husband: What is wrong with my knee? "I hear this little click when I'm walking. And there's a twinge too sometimes if I take the stairs." He is eating a spoonful of peanut butter. He puts it in the sink, then kneels down to examine me. "Does this hurt?" he asks, pressing lightly on the skin. "How about this? Or this?" I waggle my hand to indicate maybe it does, maybe a little bit. He stands up and gives me a kiss. "Knee cancer?" he says.

One good thing about being addicted to sleeping pills is that they don't call it "addicted"; they call it "habituated."

■ ■ ■ ■

Funny how people will lecture you about anything these days. This one on the library steps is going on and on about my ham sandwich. "Pigs are more trainable than dogs! Cows understand cause and effect!" Who asked you anyway? I think, but I leave and eat it at my desk.

But the man in the shabby suit tells me things I want to know. He works for hospice. He said that it is important when a loved one dies to try to stay alone in the house for three days. This is when the manifestations occur. His wife manifested as a small whirlwind that swept the papers off his desk. Marvelous, marvelous, he said.

■ ■ ■ ■

There's a sign on our elevator saying it is out of order. I stand there looking at it as if it might change. Mrs. Kovinski comes into the lobby. They'll let anyone be super now, is her theory. Anyone.

I get the mail, put off making my slow way up the stairs. The fancy preschool still sends us the newsletter. This one features a list of the top ten fears reported by their students. Darkness doesn't make the cut. Blood, sharks, and loneliness are 8, 9, and 10.

When I come in, the dog is sleeping under the table. Eli is folding a piece of plain white paper. "Don't look," he says. "I'm inventing this. No one will ever know what I have done except me."

I don't look. I put out kibble and water, peer openheartedly into the fridge. The window is open. It's nice out. The pigeons aren't on the fire escape. There are some pots left over from the tomato experiment. "Whoosh," my son says.

My #1 fear is the acceleration of days. No

such thing supposedly, but I swear I can feel it.

■ ■ ■ ■

"Do you want a snack?" she asks me. I hesitate because Catherine works in advertising. She met my brother when he signed up to be in a focus group for her agency. A hundred dollars cash was the pay. The assignment was to brainstorm names for a new deodorant aimed at children under ten. The Stink of Angels was his contribution.

I still can't quite believe they're a couple, but on their first date, they both ordered club soda. Twelve Steppers call it the Thirteenth Step. She used to do a little coke. He was all about the pills.

I tell Catherine I'm just going to wait for dinner. Later, I cruise by her desk and, sure enough, there's a folder there.

Potato Chips: Ambitious, successful, high achiever

Nuts: Easygoing, empathetic, understanding

Popcorn: Takes charge, smart, self-confident

I head into the living room and there is Ben, blithely eating cashews.

■ ■ ■ ■

Sunday morning. The dog has found a baby bunny in the grass. She closed her mouth around it once, then released it. Now we are trying to save it. Someone at the community garden has given us a box lined with a soft cloth. But it is trembling violently. There is no blood anywhere, but there are small indents in the fur that show where her teeth have been. We try to put it back in the garden but it has already died. Of fright, I think.

That night, Eli calls to us hysterically from the kitchen. There's a mouse skull under the sink, he says. I give Ben a dark look. We are killing them secretly, I thought. Heavily, he rises to go in there. He gets down on his knees to look under the sink. But it is only a knob of ginger and we are saved.

■ ■ ■ ■

I don't know what to do about this car service man. He told me business is down; no one is calling anymore. He had to let all his drivers go and is down to one car. He sleeps at work now so as to never miss a call. His wife has said she is going to leave him.

Mr. Jimmy. That's the name on the card he gave me. I try to use only his service now, not the better, faster one. Sometimes when I call his voice is groggy. He says always that he will be there in seven minutes, but it is much longer now.

I used to take a car service only if I was going to be late, but now I find I am building in double the amount of travel time. A bus would be the same or faster. Also, I could afford it. But what if I am the only customer he has left?

I'm late for the lecture now. And I was wrong about which building it's in. By the time I get there, Sylvia is almost through speaking. There's a big crowd. Behind her is a graph shaped like a hockey stick.

"What it means to be a good person, a moral person, is calculated differently in times of crisis than in ordinary circumstances," she says. She pulls up a slide of people having a picnic by a lake. Blue skies, green trees, white people.

"Suppose you go with some friends to the park to have a picnic. This act is, of course, morally neutral, but if you witness a group of children drowning in the lake and you continue to eat and chat, you have become monstrous."

The moderator makes a gesture to show it is time to wrap up. A line of men is forming behind the microphone. "I have both a question *and* a comment," they say. A young woman stands up to wait in line. I watch as she inches forward. Finally, she makes it to the front to ask her question.

"How do you maintain your optimism?"

I can't get to Sylvia afterward. There are too many people. I walk to the subway, trying to think about the world.

Young person worry: What if nothing I do matters?

Old person worry: What if everything I do does?

■ ■ ■ ■

For almost two years, I have managed not to run into this mother from the old pre-school. At times, it takes some doing. I definitely have to be eagle-eyed if I venture into the fancy bakery or the co-op. Her name is Nicola and her son's name, inexplicably, is Kasper.

She had this way that she would talk about our zoned elementary school, in one breath praising the immigrant kids who went there and in the next talking about the tutors she'd hired to get her son out of it. Strivers, she called them. Like they were all cleaning chimneys or selling papers hot off the press.

Nicola used to carry flash cards with her, and she'd greet her son at pickup with a snack that she said the name of in another language. *Pomme. Banane.*

Eli was enamored with her. He wanted me to wear nicer clothes. He wanted me to teach him the foreign names of fruit. One day I brought him an orange (in French: *orange*). I told him he could take the test if he wanted, but that there would be, of course, no pricey tutors.

A few days later, I yelled at him for losing his new lunch box, and he turned to me and said, Are you sure you're my mother? Sometimes you don't seem like a good enough person.

He was just a kid, so I let it go. And now, years later, I probably only think of it, I don't know, once or twice a day.

■ ■ ■ ■

I finally tried the meditation class. My knee was hurting so I sat on a chair. The mostly enlightened woman was there on a cushion. I'd wondered what happened to her. At the end, she asked Margot a question or what she seemed to think was a question.

"I have been fortunate enough to spend a great deal of time in the melted ego world. But I find I have trouble coming back to the differentiated world, the one you were just talking about where you have to wash the dishes and take out the garbage."

She was very pregnant, six months maybe. Oh, don't worry, I thought, the differentiated world is coming for your ass.

■ ■ ■ ■

As it turned out, Eli did fine on that test. Not well enough for the citywide schools, but well enough to be placed in something the district called EAGLE. (They never said what it stood for, but who cares, because, duh, eagles soar!) For Nicola, though, all of this was the culmination of a year's work. I remember how she came in beaming the day after the results. We've had quite a week, she told me. We've just learned that Kasper is gifted *and* talented.

Oh my, I said.

Soon after that he came over to our house for a playdate. The boys played Legos, then ran around jumping on and off different things. They were soldiers, ninjas, nothing particularly surprising or revealing of hidden depths. But then Eli took out his favorite toy, which was a set of plastic ice-cream cones and scoops. He asked his friend if he wanted to play ice-cream truck, but Kasper crouched under the table and played his own game. It was called Time, he said.

What is better when you are older?

Picnics.

Picnics?

People bring better things.

■ ■ ■ ■

Sylvia comes by the library. "I have a proposal for you," she says. She wants to pay me to answer her email. There's a lot of it these days because of the podcast. She's been answering it herself, but she can't keep up anymore.

I ask her what sorts of things she gets. All kinds, she tells me, but everyone who writes her is either crazy or depressed. We need the money for sure, but I tell her I have to think about it. Because it's possible my life is already filled with these people.

■ ■ ■ ■

It's the first day of spring, weird clouds, hazy sun. Henry is doing that looping thing he does. He's always been like this, but he's good at hiding it from other people. He saves up everything until we're together, then he starts in with the confessions.

"I keep having this thought, Lizzie."

"What thought?"

"What if I sold my soul to the devil when I was a kid?"

"You didn't sell your soul to the devil."

"What if I did but I don't remember it?"

"You didn't sell your soul to the devil."

"But what if I did?"

"Okay, but think, Henry, what did you get for it?"

■ ■ ■ ■

A few days later, Sylvia decides to improve her offer. She says I could travel with her too, keep track of things, help her through the boring bits. One caveat: the mail has been skewing evangelical lately. Lots of questions about the Rapture mixed in with the ones about wind turbines and carbon taxes. "No problem," I tell her. "Trip down memory lane." Her mistake was calling her show *Hell and High Water.* Guaranteed to attract the end-timers.

I flip through a folder full of questions people have sent her. She has printed them out like an old person, which I guess is what she is.

Is the Insectothopter like the AlphaCheetah? Does extinction matter since we know how the Bible ends? Who invented contrails? How will the last generation know it is the last generation?

She looks tired, I think, a little blurred around the edges. She's been on this never-ending speaking tour. I should help her. I say yes, okay, why not, sure.

■ ■ ■ ■

The problem with Eli's school is it's not on a human scale. Five stories tall. A dozen first grade classes. When the bell rings, the teachers march the kids out in strict little lines. The playground is big, but it backs out onto the avenue. There is a hole in the fence where the wire is bent, and every time I see it I feel a jolt of dread. All year, I've been on some soul-crushing committee where we talk about getting it fixed. I'm not a joiner, but believe me, I work less than these immigrant parents.

So I wrote letter after letter to the board of ed. *It has come to our attention . . .* Nothing happened. I heard there was one committee that spent an entire year trying to get seedlings into the kindergarten classrooms. In the end, no. Denied. A safety issue, they said.

■ ■ ■ ■

Lately, I've observed that I dress like the kids on campus or maybe they dress like me. I have dressed the same way a long time, but somehow it has cycled in again. I'm old enough now that I sometimes think about how I am making a fool of myself by doing something that would not have attracted notice when I was younger. So at the beginning of the year I went out and bought some new, plainer things. Henry says I'm dressing like a little dun bird.

Q: How is the goodness of God manifested even in the clothing of birds and beasts?

A: Small birds, which are the most delicate, have more feathers than those that are hardier. Beasts that live in the icy regions have thicker, coarser coats than those that dwell in the tropical heat.

I need to pack for this trip, but there's something buzzing around the room. I can't see it, but I can hear it hurling itself against the glass. A bee maybe, or a wasp. Over there, on the blinds, I think. I capture it with the aid of a cup and an index card.

Quiet in the cup. Hard to believe that isn't joy, the way it flies away when I fling it out the window.

■ ■ ■

Still light when we come out of the theater. Henry's off to see Catherine. He's meeting her friends from the ad agency. The Creatives, she calls them, because she's not one; she's one of the Suits. I like the sound of it. Like there might be a rumble later.

But I can tell Henry's nervous. "Just remember, don't be yourself," I say. He laughs a little. I watch him walk off, hands in his pockets, slumped over. *Stick together, you two.* That's what my mother used to say.

I remember the first time I made him dinner. I took the chicken from the fridge and peeled off the disgusting, filmy wrapper. Pink juice got everywhere, but I wiped it up with a sponge. Then I put the chicken in a pan and poured a bottle of soy sauce over it. Fifteen minutes later, we ate it.

Everything

Material   Immaterial

Animate   Inanimate

Sensible   Insensible

I listen to *Hell and High Water* on the way
home. This one is about Deep Time. The
geologist being interviewed speaks quickly,
sweeping through millions and millions of
years in a moment. The Age of Birds has
passed, he says. Also of Reptiles. Also of
Flowering Plants. Holocene was the name
of our age. Holocene, which meant "now."

■ ■ ■ ■

First conference with Sylvia. One thing I'll
say about it: lots of people who are not Native Americans talking about Native Americans.

The Shuswap region was considered by
the local tribes to be a beautiful and plenti-

ful land. There were salmon and game in the warm months and tubers and roots in the cold ones. The tribes that lived there developed various technologies to help them make use of all of their resources. For many years, in this way, they prospered beautifully on their land. But the elders saw that the tribes' world had become too predictable and the challenge had gone out of life. Without challenge, they counseled, life had no meaning. So after a few decades, their custom was to advise that the entire village be moved to another place. All of them went to a different part of the Shuswap territory and by starting over life regained its meaning. There were new streams to figure out, new game trails to learn. Everyone felt rejuvenated.

This person has done something similar. For a long time, she lived in San Francisco, and now she has moved to Portland.

■ ■ ■ ■

Sometimes I like to ask my boss about little patterns I notice at the library. She has worked here for twenty years. She sees everyone and everything. So how come three different people came in today and wanted to put up flyers about beekeeping? But this time Lorraine just shrugs. "Some things are in the air, they float around," she says, and I think of leaves, of something falling and accumulating without notice.

Also in the air: a coworker who has taken to carrying X-rays around in her purse. Some kind of medical mistake. It can't be undone, but it can be recounted.

Then there's that professor who was always golden, the one who got tenure right away. Suddenly he's not a drinker but a drunk. Last week, he had to be carried out of his own birthday party and put into a taxi. They had to pay the driver in advance or he wouldn't have taken him. It wasn't the first time either, Lorraine said. And soon the party is for me.

I do have one bookish superstition about my birthday. I like to see what Virginia Woolf said about an age in her diaries before I reach it. Usually it's inspiring.

Other times . . .

> Life is as I've said since I was 10, awfully interesting — if anything, quicker, keener at 44 than 24 — more desperate I suppose, as the river shoots to Niagara — my new vision of death; active, positive, like all the rest, exciting; & of great importance — as an experience.

■ ■ ■ ■

I buy a telescope because I want to see. I buy running shoes because I want to run. This block smells like garbage. Turn left for greener streets. Yes, better. I try to run all the way to the park, but these shoes don't work.

■ ■ ■ ■

I don't tell Ben much about these letters. He would not be pleased by the nature of these questions. He's already worried the evangelicals are trying to take over everything. In cahoots, of course, with the Jews for Jesus.

There's that one who parks himself by the Dunkin' Donuts on weekends. "Excuse me, did you know that Jesus Christ was Jewish?" he asks us when we pass. "Yup," we tell him.

Also, we have heard the Good News. As has everyone on the whole planet, including those hunter-gatherers who live deep in the rain forest and were trying for no contact. Just once I wish someone would say that and the Good News would turn out to be something else.

■ ■ ■ ■

There's a note on the fridge saying we are out of milk, cheese, bread, and toilet paper. I tell Eli I will take him out to eat at the diner. NO ANIMALS ALLOWED, the sign outside the restaurant reads. "But we are animals, right?" "Don't be a stickler," I tell him.

Eli announces that he has decided to have two children; no, he corrects himself, one, because it is easier. We order grilled cheese sandwiches and eavesdrop on the people at the next table. "Is he your soul mate?" the woman asks her friend. "Hard to tell," she says.

■ ■ ■ ■

When are the Days of Tribulation? Did Noah's flood cover the whole earth or just the places where people lived? Can pets be saved in Christ and go to heaven? If not, what will happen to them?

We used to worry most about the last one. We had a cat that my mother allowed us to name jointly. Stacy Stormbringer was the result, and we were devoted to her. But then we saw that movie at Bible camp. The father was raptured up and all that was left behind was his electric razor buzzing. Our mother was definitely saved, but were we really? What if we came home and the house was empty? Would we at least have Stacy Stormbringer?

Swept up, they called it. As if God were a broom.

■ ■ ■ ■

Henry and Catherine come over for dinner. She brings giant sunflowers and I try to find a vase to hold them. She seems unnerved by all the books. "Have you read all of these?" she asks me. Later, she starts a conversation based on the idea that we're living in unprecedented times.

I can see Ben hesitate. He has a complicated relationship to modern things. On the one hand, he makes educational video games. On the other, he has a PhD in classics. Two bad years on the job market and then he quit and learned to code.

I decide to comment for him. I recount some half-baked story about Lucretius. This guy lived in the first century BCE but claimed that in his time there was too much bored rushing around. Terrible fears one minute! Apathy the next! Catherine looks at Henry and then at me. "I just meant politics," she says.

■ ■ ■ ■

Sometimes Mr. Jimmy speaks in little bursts. Today he tells me about how he'd taken his son's old car across the river to a junkyard, where giant machines crushed it. "You should have seen it," he says. He told me he tried to lift up the little bit of the metal that was left, but it was too heavy and it wouldn't move an inch. "But these things lifted it up like it was nothing!" I tell him one day those machines are going to come and crush all of us. He likes that. Smiles a little. "It'll just be like a big claw coming," he says.

■ ■ ■ ■

Sylvia takes me to a swanky dinner with some people visiting from Silicon Valley. Some of them are donors to her podcast and she hopes to convince them to support a new foundation she has started. It wants to rewild half the earth.

But these men are not interested in such things. De-extinction is a better route, they think. Already they are exploring the genetic engineering that would be necessary. Woolly mammoths are of great interest to them. Saber-tooth tigers too.

Somehow, I get seated halfway down the table from her. I'm trapped next to this young techno-optimist guy. He explains that current technology will no longer seem strange when the generation who didn't grow up with it finally ages out of the conversation. Dies, I think he means.

His point is that eventually all those who are unnerved by what is falling away will be gone, and after that, there won't be any more talk of what has been lost, only of what has been gained.

But wait, that sounds bad to me. Doesn't that mean if we end up somewhere we don't want to be, we can't retrace our steps?

He ignores this, blurs right past me to list all the ways he and his kind have changed the world and will change the world. He tells me that smart houses are coming, that soon everything in our lives will be hooked up to the internet of things, blah, blah, blah, and we will be connected through social media to every other person in the world. He asks me what my favored platforms are.

I explain that I don't use any of them because they make me feel too squirrelly. Or not exactly squirrelly, more like a rat who can't stop pushing a lever.

Pellet of affection! Pellet of rage! Please, please, my pretty!

He looks at me and I can see him calculating all the large and small ways I am trying to prevent the future. "Well, good luck with that, I guess," he says.

Later, Sylvia tells me her end of the table was even worse. The guy in the Gore-Tex jacket was going on and on about transhumanism and how we would soon shed these burdensome bodies and become part of the singularity. "These people long for immortality but can't wait ten minutes for a cup of coffee," she says.

■ ■ ■ ■

A new member of the meditation class tells a story about going to a monastery. He says that the atmosphere was incredible, like nothing he had ever experienced. Margot looks at him. "It is only the people who visit the monastery who feel anything. The people in the monastery feel nothing," she says. I can't help it. I laugh. "Sit straighter," she says to me, and her voice is like a sharp stick.

■ ■ ■ ■

Okay, okay, I have officially wrecked my knee with all this gallivanting around. Last night, the pain was so bad I couldn't sleep. Ben insists I get it checked out this week. But before I go, I have some questions. Like what if it's gout? "It is definitely not gout," he tells me. "Could it be arthritis? I'm too young for that, right?" He nods. "You are way too young, plus that comes much more slowly."

That night, I dream that I am in a supermarket. Bad music is playing. It's pitilessly lit. I walk up and down the aisles, trying to dim the lights, but I can't find the switch. I wake up, disappointed. What happened to the flying dreams?

■ ■ ■ ■

On the way there, Mr. Jimmy has questions for me. What are these shows about, really? Is there a takeaway message? No, I tell him. But actually there is.

First, they came for the coral, but I did not say anything because I was not a coral . . .

At the clinic, the doctor manipulates my knee. He asks me if I have any other conditions. "Such as?" "Gout?" "How would I know if I had gout?" I say, my voice rising weirdly. "Oh, you'd know," he says. He sends me in for X-rays.

The technician is older than me, relentlessly cheerful, joking about how she can barely stand up after repositioning the machine. "Don't laugh at the broken-down old tech," she says. "I'm fine. Don't laugh at me." I worry that she is modeling something for me, some sort of way I am supposed to deal with adversity and affliction. "No chance of being pregnant," she says. Not as a question. She puts the heavy lead apron around my waist anyway.

I stand three different ways. The last one is like a yoga pose, hurt leg bent and forward, the other straight. A wave of pain and nausea hits me. I stand back up, blinking hard. She is still behind the glass, chattering at me. She sends me back into the little room to wait.

The doctor comes back after a while. "Good

news," he says. "Nothing to worry about." I go home with a piece of paper. *Osteoarthritis, minor degeneration,* it says. I look it up on the train.

> Osteoarthritis develops slowly and the pain it causes worsens over time.

Right, okay, steady on. Later, when I tell Ben the gout story, my voice is less jaunty than I intend. I make a little joke and the room steadies. But I saw his eyes. I know what he's remembering. That time the dog's muzzle went gray.

■ ■ ■ ■

Henry doesn't seem to notice I'm hobbling a little. He is filling me in on the new job Catherine got him. He's a copywriter now for some low-rent greeting card company. It's those kinds of cards that are very long and very specific about all the things the recipient has done for the sender.

To a Step-Aunt Who Was Always
    There . . .
To a Hospitalized Second Cousin . . .

Sometimes they rhyme, but mostly they are free verse. Henry gets paid by the word, so the more flowery the better. Even so, he already got into an argument with his boss about the difference between sentiment and sentimentality.

You have to kiss the ring, Catherine said.

■ ■ ■ ■

In the morning, the adjunct comes by to say hello. He looks pale. I worry he is selling his plasma again. He tells me that his classroom was locked yesterday and he had to wait in the hallway for an hour until someone finally came to open it. By then all his students had left. But he tells me he is getting better at handling such things. At first, it was unnerving to work somewhere

where no one remembers your name, where you have to call security to get into your own room, but as regular life becomes more fragmented and bewildering, it bothers him less and less, he says.

Q: What is the philosophy of late capitalism?

A: Two hikers see a hungry bear on the trail ahead of them. One of them takes out his running shoes and puts them on. "You can't outrun a bear," the other whispers. "I just have to outrun you," he says.

When I get home, Eli is watching audition tapes of those people who want to go on a one-way trip to Mars. This one has found a brand-new way, never before used in history, to skip out on his wife and kids. It's difficult, of course, to consider leaving his family forever and never meeting his future grandchildren. But he's intrigued by the idea of making history and seeing things no one has ever seen before. His wife and children don't like the idea much. They are afraid they will have to watch him die on television.

Breathing in, I know that I am of the nature to grow old.

Breathing out, I know that I cannot escape old age.

Breathing in, I know that I am of the nature to get sick.

Breathing out, I know that I cannot escape sickness.

Breathing in, I know that I am of the nature to die.

Breathing out, I know that I cannot escape dying.

Breathing in, I know that one day I will have to let go of everything and everyone I love.

Breathing out, I know there is no way to bring them along.

Aw, c'mon, man. Everything and everyone I love? Is there one for beginners maybe?

■ ■ ■ ■

That drug dealer who lives in 5C always surprises me. He's big and sleepy-eyed, but his reflexes are lightning quick. Today a grocery bag I was carrying broke, and he caught the glass bottle of oil before it hit. He has a baby girl who doesn't live with him, a beautiful dog, and a small jagged scar on his neck. Once I asked if he grew up in the neighborhood and he smiled and shook his head. I just kind of bounced around as a kid, he told me. A little bit here, a little bit there.

■ ■ ■ ■

Another conference, this one in the heart-
land. Sylvia gives a lecture while I sit in the
front row, holding her purse like a proper
assistant. She talks about a book called *Nature and Silence.* There is no higher or
lower, it says. Everything is equally evolved.

Sylvia tells the audience that the only reason
we think humans are the height of evolution
is that we have chosen to privilege certain
things above other things. For example, if
we privileged the sense of smell, dogs would
be deemed more evolved. After all, they
have about three hundred million olfactory
receptors in their noses compared with our
six million. If we privileged longevity, it
would be bristlecone pines, which can live
for several thousand years. And you could
make a case that banana slugs are sexually
superior to us. They are hermaphrodites
who mate up to three times a day.

There are a lot of questions afterward. Some
of them are friendly; some are not. But Sylvia stands firm on her idea that humans are

nothing particularly special. "The only thing we are demonstrably better at than other animals is sweating and throwing," she says.

Now I'm on a park bench, noting the scattered lettuce of someone else's sandwich. I clean it up, then resent doing it. On the way back, I don't notice anything underfoot, anything overhead. Possibly there was a light coming greenly through the leaves. Impossible to be sure.

What is the Nano Hummingbird? What is the Robofish?

■ ■ ■ ■

When I get home, the dog is in the kitchen, tearing a rawhide bone into slobbery bits. My mother told me once that each thing, each being, has two names. One is the name by which it is known in this world and the other is a secret name that it keeps hidden. But if you call it by this name it cannot help but respond. This is the name by which the creature was known in the Garden of Eden.

61

Later, I spend some time trying to find out the dog's secret name, but she's not having it.

■ ■ ■

The first reading of the year is the newly sober English professor. He has been writing poetry at rehab. One of them is from the point of view of a hat being worn by a beautiful woman. After he reads it, he directs some remarks to his students in attendance. "I have written about a hat though I have never been a hat," he says. Later, as we are boxing up the unsold books, I find a card someone has left for him.

You've received this card because your privilege is showing.

Your words/actions are making others feel uncomfortable.

CHECK YOUR PRIVILEGE.

[√] White   [√] Heterosexual
[√] Male   [√] Neuro-typical
[√] Socioeconomic   [√] Citizen

"What do you think this is?" he asks me.

The future?

■ ■ ■ ■

And the lonely heart engineer wants to downsize the government. A desire for a small government is nothing new, of course. At the end of the nineteenth century, a U.S. government official proposed closing the office of patents. Everything of importance had already been invented, he said.

Ben is reading a book about pre-Socratic philosophy. I've always had an obsession with lost books, all the ones half written or recovered in pieces. So today in my lunch, I find a sandwich, a cookie, and a note from him.

Ostensibly there is color, ostensibly sweetness, ostensibly bitterness, actually only atoms and the void.

(Democritus wrote seventy books. Only fragments survive.)

■ ■ ■ ■

I really need to unpack this suitcase. Are you trying to tell me something? Ben asked last night as he stepped over it again. We have these little Are you leaving me? jokes. The oldest one goes like this:

Be right back, I'm going out for a pack of cigarettes, the man tells his wife.

(Years pass.)

■ ■ ■ ■

I swear the hippie letters are a hundred

times more boring than the end-timer ones. They are all about composting toilets and water conservation and electric cars and how to live lightly on the earth while thinking ahead for seven generations. "Environmentalists are so dreary," I tell Sylvia. "I know, I know," she says.

■ ■ ■ ■

Outside the library, the woman who is always on the bench is talking about Thanksgiving. She's had enough, she doesn't want to go anymore, she tells someone. It's May, but I think she's smart to plan ahead. She has long gray hair, a briefcase filled with papers. There are various stories about who she used to be. Grad student still working on her dissertation is a popular one. But my boss says she once worked in the cafeteria. I try to slip by her bench unnoticed, but she stops her conversation to ask me for money. I don't have the usual dollar, just some coins and a twenty. Once in a fluster I gave her a ten, and ever since I've been a disappointment to her. I dig out some change from my pocket. She takes a careful look at the nickels and dimes. God blesses me anyway.

■ ■ ■ ■

One night, Ben's mother calls from Florida, a.k.a. paradise. She wants to be buried there, she says. And she's talked his father into it too. But there's a problem. They already bought grave plots by their old synagogue. Could we maybe sell them to someone else for her? "I don't know how we'd do that, Mom," he says. She offers that we could take them ourselves, but Ben doesn't want to be buried in Hackensack, New Jersey.

I think of the time Sylvia interviewed that famous futurist. She asked him what was coming next, and he repeated his best-known prediction: *Old people, in big cities, afraid of the sky.*

■ ■ ■ ■

Some of the people at this private dinner have begun to invest in floating cities, the kind that can be anchored in international waters and run by unmeddlesome governments, but our hosts are gentler sorts, longtime listeners, they say. They take notes during Sylvia's talk, but in the end they still have one nagging question: What will be the safest place? No one they'd consulted with would give them a straight answer.

"But you've interviewed everyone. Is there any consensus? Any clustering patterns of these scientists and journalists? We're not asking for ourselves, but we have children, you understand."

■ ■ ■ ■

Catherine has made us a wholesome vegetarian dinner to celebrate that Henry is moving in. He lost his lease because the landlord's son wants his apartment. If he had told her earlier, she would have helped him fight it, but he waited until the last minute.

I understand his reluctance. The moment you tell Catherine about a problem she begins to act and she does not stop acting until the problem is solved. For this reason, my brother sometimes lets a problem go on for some time before telling her about it in order to prepare himself for the intensity of her mobilization.

But it's probably for the best, because here he is, bright-eyed and clean-shaven, serving us some kind of thing made of bulgur wheat. There are placemats and candlesticks too. I want to joke about how he is moving up in the world, but I resist. All this order is good for him maybe.

For dessert, Catherine serves fruit with unsweetened whipped cream. My son rips his napkin into smaller and smaller pieces. "What is there to do here?" he whispers. Henry overhears and leans in to speak softly in his ear. Eli smiles.

"What did you tell him?" I ask my brother later. "I told him nothing," he says.

■ ■ ■ ■

This woman has just turned fifty. She tells me about her blurriness, the way she is hardly seen. She supposes she is not so pretty anymore — fattish, hair a bit gray. What she has noticed, what gives her a little chill, she tells me, is how if she meets a man out of the context of work, he finds her to not be worth much. He looks over her shoulder as he talks or pawns her off on a woman her own age. "I have to be so careful now," she says.

■ ■ ■ ■

Eli and I are looking over his homework, which is mostly xeroxed worksheets. His social studies book was published twenty years ago. It's called *Lands and Peoples.* "We always say Native American!" Eli says. "Never Indian. I thought Amira was an Indian, from India, but she is Bangladeshi."

This is the girl he loves. They are both

EAGLEs. I tell him that in the reports they sent back from the New World, the colonists claimed there were spiders as big as cats and birds as small as thimbles. They wrote that there were flora and fauna so strange they dared not try to describe them. But this is not of interest to him. "Yes, Amira is from Bangladesh," I say, on firm ground again.

That night on the show, there's an expert giving advice about how to survive disasters, natural and man-made. He says it's a myth that people panic in emergencies. Eighty percent just freeze. The brain refuses to take in what is happening. This is called the incredulity response. "Those who live move," he says.

■ ■ ■ ■

That's Nicola outside the bakery. She's on her phone, but as soon as she looks up, she'll see me. I dart through the doorway just in time. She's put her phone away and is striding purposefully down the street. But I'm safe in the hardware store.

Actually, a mistake, because now the owner wants to tell me all about the old days in Flatbush. Things have changed. The neighborhood has changed. New people keep moving in from other places. They don't understand the way things are done. They've got no patience. Sometimes they don't even know the name of what they are asking for.

He goes on describing me and my ilk. Possibly I will have to buy something to get out of here. I've gotten trapped once before, trying to buy blue masking tape. And this man tells the most depressing stories; even when you think a story won't be like that, he finds a way.

But now this man is telling me how much he loves his store, how he could list every nail and screw he carries. Ever since he was a boy, he has liked the look of them, the way the weight of a good tool feels in your hand. But the people who come in nowadays, they're used to the chain stores. They don't care about service. They don't care about expertise. And their understanding of inventory is unrealistic. "If you want Home Depot, go to Home Depot!" he says.

I buy the cheapest hammer in the store and he lets me out of there.

■ ■ ■ ■

It is dusk when Henry and I leave the park. A car nearly runs us over. Now we're right next to her at the light. My brother goes up to the window. "Lady, you almost killed us," he tells her. But she won't look at him. "You and your precious lives," she says.

Later, I tell the story to Margot.
"You talk about your brother a great deal," she observes.
"We're close."
"That's not the word I'd use."
"What's the word?"
"Enmeshed," she says.

■ ■ ■

This one's daughter was an addict. She always had Narcan on her in case she had to revive her. Then for a long time she didn't come in. Now she is telling me about the day her daughter OD'd. "I went to the grocery store," she says. "I went to the grocery store for one minute." She wants to pay her fines, months and months of them, but I pretend there aren't any.

Last week, we got trained to use it. And when that person comes to, do you think they will be happy you saved their life? the facilitator asked. No, not at all, was the correct answer.

Do you ever take on the burdens of others? is question five on the enmeshment questionnaire.

■ ■ ■ ■

Eli won't stop fidgeting tonight. He tips his

chair back and forth until I get mad at him. Then he gets up to sharpen his pencil. "I wish it were winter," he mutters. There is a prompt at the bottom, reminding him to answer the question in a complete sentence.

Eskimos live in very cold countries. We make our houses out of wood or bricks. The Eskimo makes his house out of snow. There is little wood in his cold country. Can a snow house keep him warm?

"Isn't it Inuit?" I say. "Eskimo is an old word, I think." He isn't listening to me really. Later, I go looking through my books to see if I can find what I'm remembering. And then, just when I'm about to give up, there it is in a box of my old papers. I wrote half a dissertation once. "The Domestication of Death: Cross-Cultural Mythologies," I was pleased to call it.

I wait until bedtime. Eli and I have this routine that is always the same. Just before he's drifting off he'll tell me about his day. Then he'll close his eyes, crush my hand in his, and say, "Happy thought?"

When Houses Were Alive

One night a house suddenly rose up from the ground and went floating through the air. It was dark, & it is said that a swishing, rushing noise was heard as it flew through the air. The house had not yet reached the end of its road when the people inside begged it to stop. So the house stopped.

They had no blubber when they stopped. So they took soft, freshly drifted snow & put it in their lamps, & it burned.

They had come down at a village. A man came to their house & said: Look, they are burning snow in their lamps. Snow can burn.

But the moment these words were uttered, the lamp went out.

(as told by Inugpasugjuk)

■ ■ ■ ■

Exams are over, but there are still a few students lingering on campus. A girl whose name I forget comes into the library to shoot the breeze. She has brought me one of those healthy juices she likes to drink. It tastes like a shake made of cut grass. There is powdered bee pollen in it too and this allegedly protects the drinker from all manner of ruinous things.

She tells me that her phone was stolen and she's been using a really old one instead. She won't get the newest model, she's decided. "So I just go at a slower pace. I know I'm missing things because I can't respond quickly enough to what people say or show me, but that's okay. It gives me more time to think," she says.

I am charmed by her. She seems practically like a transcendentalist. I take another sip of her grass drink and think maybe it is giving me some kind of burst of energy.

She takes out her phone to demonstrate its obsolescence to me. It is exactly the same kind as mine. Mine is two years old but still retrieves things for me in the blink of an eye.

"Wait," I say. "Were you talking about seconds? When you said you were so out of step and living slowly, did you mean by seconds?" She considers this. "Yeah," she says, "seconds probably."

I take the car service home because I'm ridiculous. Mr. Jimmy is complaining about how "that company" is ruining his business. For some reason he won't say the name, but I know who he is talking about. He came over here from Ireland as a teenager; twenty-five years he's been driving, he says. "They don't even check out the people they use. It's just anyone with a semi-new car." I have heard this, I tell him. There is even some case where a passenger said the driver assaulted her. He gives me a quick look. "Right," he says. "No standards."

Later, I remember to tell Ben about the girl. "Seconds!" I say, but he is unmoved. "People always talk about email and phones and how they alienate us from one another, but these sorts of fears about technology have always been with us," he claims.

When electricity was first introduced to

homes, there were letters to the newspapers about how it would undermine family togetherness. Now there would be no need to gather around a shared hearth, people fretted. In 1903, a famous psychologist worried that young people would lose their connection to dusk and its contemplative moments.

Hahaha!

(Except when was the last time I stood still because it was dusk?)

■ ■ ■ ■

It's my birthday tomorrow. "Now you are officially middle-aged," says my coworker who carries around the X-rays. She has never liked me because I don't have a proper degree. Feral librarians, they call us, as in just wandered out of the woods.

Lorraine has organized an after-work celebration. We go to that bar where I used to work. It's called the Burrow and it's well named. Dark and small and warm. And my friend Tracy is here to pour us extra stiff drinks. I decide to drink gimlets because it's more festive.

We catch up a little. She is six months into dating a handsome, horrible guy who lives in Philadelphia. She details his moments of cruelty, punctuating the story with little laughs. "And then I drove all the way there to see him even though it terrifies me to drive in traffic."

When she got there, he had left a note on the door saying he had to go out of town unexpectedly. *Let yourself in,* the note said, but he'd only talked of, never followed through with, giving her a key.

"You need someone kind," I say.

Something in her eyes then, something hard to read. Finally, it registers. She feels sorry for me and for all the rest who have thrown in their lot with kindness and decency.

"Sure, sure, I suppose I could go for someone safe," she says. "But I've never felt like this before. Never."

But no one is safe, I want to tell her. *Safe?*

When we worked together years ago, she always told me I had no game. She said this because allegedly you are not supposed to cut to the chase and ask your fellow dater to tell you about the time he was most soul-crushingly lonely. Allegedly this is not a best practice. But it makes a date so much less boring. Do you, did you, will you? I just want to know.

I offer her some birthday cake. She goes into the usual bit about temptation and sinfulness and maybe this and maybe that, and we have to go through every station of the fucking cross before she takes a bite of it. "That was delicious," she says, then hustles off to make some drinks. I'm on number five, I think. Maybe six.

Let's pause here.

But I don't, I don't. Now I'm talking to everyone at the bar. I'm telling stories, good ones at first, then not so good as the night wears on. If only I'd remembered that old proverb:

When three people say you are drunk, go to sleep.

Because the fact that there are six thousand miles of New York sewers and all of them lie well below sea level has become my go-to conversational gambit.

In the morning, my head is pounding. There is a tableful of presents. There are waffles with strawberries and whipped cream. Also, Ben stayed up late sharpening pencils he found under the couch. He set aside the nicest ones for me. I am pleased to put them in my backpack. Especially this red one I thought I'd never see again.

■ ■ ■ ■

Mr. Jimmy notices I am limping. He tells

81

me that his adult son became disabled through no fault of his own. "No fault of his own," he repeats. "It breaks your heart," he says, and I agree.

I try to reach Sylvia as I wait for the bell. "I have to call you back," she says. "I'm about to send off this article, but I have to come up with the obligatory note of hope."

It's stupidly hot out. I stand there, sweating in my black T-shirt. Amira's mother is right next to me. You have to try, Eli told me yesterday. You have to ask. It's almost summer and he's getting scared. How will he see her? Where does she even live?

But I don't know the name of Amira's mother. And she is talking to her friend in a language I don't speak. There are four days left of school, three minutes until the bell rings. I put my earbuds in and listen to an episode about something called the "mesh." It's a better term than "web," they think.

A man calls in from Dallas. *What do you mean interconnected?* he says. There is a pause and then the ecologist speaks: *There is a species of moth in Madagascar that drinks the tears of sleeping birds.*

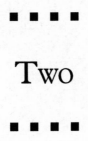

Two

Two

Someone's setting firecrackers off already. It's not even noon. The dog is being driven crazy by the sound and can only be soothed by a thousand rounds of slobber frog.

Finally, I have to stop, because my hand is slick with spit. I go to the bathroom to rinse it off. There's some antibacterial soap Ben bought last week at the dollar store. It's a bright pink. Don't use antibacterial soap! Catherine told me, because lalalalalalalalala.

Ben is cleaning out the hall closet while Eli and I sprawl in front of the air conditioner. It's Monopoly day. Yesterday was Monopoly day too. We are saving money this summer by doing less camp. So here I am, waiting some long minutes while my son debates about buying St. James Place.

Pop! Pop! Pop!

The dog growls softly on the couch. Eli buys up all the railroads. Ben skates across the floor in socks to bring us red, white, and blue Popsicles.

Voted, that we are the saints.

■ ■ ■

All Eli wants to do is watch videos about robots. But they are always a disappointment. Here is some professor from MIT explaining how this crablike thing has learned to seek light and avoid obstacles. "Go!" he tells it, and it winds through a maze to find the tiny bulb at the end.

And Mrs. Kovinski has turned her TV to full volume so she can blast away every thought in my head. She watches only two things: soap operas and the nonstop news channel. I turn on some music, drown it out a bit. *How handsome am I, right? How handsome?*

■ ■ ■ ■

It's harder to get away in the summer. But still I go on a few trips with Sylvia. One thing that's becoming clear on our travels: people are really sick of being lectured to about the glaciers.

"Listen, I've heard all about that," says this red-faced man. "But what's going to happen to the American weather?"

■ ■ ■ ■

One morning a student tells me failure is not an option and is angered when I laugh. I assume a cheerful manner. I tell her, Hey, me too, I used to have plans! Biggish ones, medium at least. She stares at me. Sorry? she says. After she goes, I slip into the bathroom, make sure I don't have lipstick on my teeth.

Sometimes now with students there are these moments when it feels like a sudden cold wind blew through. So lately I've been checking that my sweater is buttoned right, that my T-shirt isn't too weird. I'm like a woman carrying a full cup into a room of strangers, trying not to spill it.

Coulda, shoulda, woulda.

When I get home, I drop the mail on my desk without looking at it. This is my favored routine. But for some reason in the morning, Ben spots how big the pile is. He comes into the kitchen, holding a stack of things.

"What do you think will happen if you don't open the bills? Do you think someone will come and take them away?"

Survival instructors have a saying: *Get organized or die.*

I have to go to work, says he, says me, says everybody.

"They keep leaving Chinese newspapers on my steps and I'm not Chinese," Mrs. Kovinski yells down the hallway.

Using the following scale, CIRCLE a number to indicate what you miss about when you were younger and how much you miss it.

1 = Not at all, 9 = Very much.

Family
1　2　3　4　5　6　7　8　9

Not having to worry
1　2　3　4　5　6　7　8　9

Places
1　2　3　4　5　6　7　8　9

Someone you loved
1　2　3　4　5　6　7　8　9

Things you did
1　2　3　4　5　6　7　8　9

The way people were
1　2　3　4　5　6　7　8　9

Feelings you had
1　2　3　4　5　6　7　8　9

The way society was
1　2　3　4　5　6　7　8　9

Pet or pets
1　2　3　4　5　6　7　8　9

Not knowing sad or evil things
1　2　3　4　5　6　7　8　9

I'm starting to understand why all those people want to go to Mars. The guest today on the show is explaining that many scientists are in a state of barely suppressed panic about the latest data coming in. Their previous models were much too conservative. Everything is happening much faster than expected. He signs off with a small borrowed witticism.

"Many of us subscribe to the same sentiment as our colleague Sherwood Rowland. He remarked to his wife one night after coming home: "The work is going well, but it looks like it might be the end of the world.""

■ ■ ■ ■

What scares you most about the mission?
I won't be afraid of anything if I'm chosen.

What will you miss the most on Earth?
I will miss swimming the most.

■ ■ ■ ■

In Maplewood, we sit on the porch, looking at their yard. Catherine's mother says she's thinking of planting a lilac bush. Her father says the last one died, you have to pick a hardier variety. It is possible they are having a fight, but it is so quietly done that I can't be sure of it.

There is nothing to do but walk around here, so I decide to ignore my twinging knee. We walk down the street beneath the flowering trees. No one else is out except the gardeners. Legions of them on the lawns, working quietly. There is one house where a famously liberal rich person lives. On this lawn, the gardeners are allowed to play their Mexican music.

Henry makes us go farther even after everyone else goes in. Catherine asked him to marry her last week and he said yes. Her parents say he has their blessing. We walk a little in silence until we reach the edge of their neighborhood and encounter one with more modest houses. CROOK, LIAR, THIEF, says the sign in one window.

"I'm going to do it wrong," my brother tells me. "I can feel all the wrong thoughts coming. What if I mess it up?" he wants to know. He is smoking now, one cigarette after another after another. "You will be forgiven," I tell him.

■ ■ ■ ■

Somehow I have stuffed a too-full garbage bag down the chute. I am flushed with triumph as I enter the hallway. Then I see Mrs. Kovinski by the elevator. She's got a cane now. She slipped and fell while on jury duty. Funny thing is it was a slip-and-fall case, she tells me. And tells me and tells me.

Sometimes I bring her books to read. She likes mysteries, she told me. Regular-type mysteries. But this last one I gave her was no good, she says. It was all jumbled up. In it, the detective investigated the crime, tracked down every clue, interviewed every possible suspect, only to discover that he himself was the murderer.

You don't say.

■ ■ ■ ■

Catherine wrote *Self Care* on my brother's hand in black marker. This is to remind him to go outside more, to eat better food, to step away from the computer.

The problem is that when he's left to his own devices, he just watches those scenes of refugees trying to make their way to safety over and over again. They keep showing pictures of this one island that is running out of resources. The people who live there have formed their own rescue teams. The fishermen go out in their boats and pull survivors out of the water. Others bring dry clothes to the beach.

Ben told me that in Greek culture it has

96

historically been considered both a duty and an honor to take care of strangers. You can see it with the villagers. The way they go out to rescue people in their boats or bring food to the exhausted ones on the beach. In ancient times, the gods used to test mortals by arriving on their doorsteps clothed in rags to see if they would be welcomed or turned away.

Henry has bookmarked this one photograph of a man carrying his child up a hill. The caption said he had traveled with her for days on a dinghy to Greece. Then he walked with her thirty-four miles to the camp. "I don't think I could do that. I don't think I'm strong enough," Henry says. "You are not going to have to walk thirty-four miles with your child on your back," I tell him.

"But if I did," he says.

■ ■ ■ ■

Anytime I think I am a semidecent person, I remember this story someone told me once about her ex-husband. He was always late getting home. He never came home when he said he would, and I thought I knew this story before she told it, but I was wrong. It was just that he had a rule that if anyone asked him for help he would pause to see what that person needed. And then he would try to get them that thing if he could. Sometimes it was money, sometimes food; once a man needed a belt and he gave him his. The reason he was always late was that his office was next door to Penn Station. They broke up because he was a mean drunk, but still.

■ ■ ■■

"You don't really even have a job, do you?" Ben says one day when I come home early. It's true. I could be one of those people who got fired months ago but still pretends to go to work every day. You see them in the library sometimes.
"Can you put sheets on his bed?"
"I fixed the drain."
"I made corn."

I hate weddings because I cry and drink too much, but this time I get lucky. Catherine gets pregnant and they have a shotgun wedding at city hall.

Maybe I can stop having that dream now. The one where my brother shows up at my apartment and says, Lizzie, can I die here?

Because suddenly I have a sister-in-law. "Oh, don't buy that," Catherine says at the bodega. "It has Blue No. 1 in it." I look at her, pretend to read the package. "It's the only dye that is known to cross the blood-brain barrier. That's what protects the brain from toxins."

I put the package back on the shelf to see if that will end the conversation, but she has more terrible knowledge she must impart to me. "Blue No. 1 enters the fluid inside the skull, but scientists don't know what it does once it's there," she tells me. Apparently, they've done research, but they still don't understand it. "Okay," I say, "but I mean, they don't even know how aspirin works, right? There is no 'theory of aspirin.' "

■ ■ ■ ■

A woman in her forties was told by her doctor that she had to improve her health. The doctor suggested that she take up jogging and run two miles every day. He told her to call him in two weeks and tell him how she felt. Two weeks later, the woman checked in. "So how are you doing?" the doctor asked. "I feel pretty good," the woman said, "but I'm twenty-eight miles from home."

■ ■ ■ ■

If I stand far enough back in the crowd, I can hide until the kids are released. I figured this out last year. The white parents tend to come to the front and stand there like some sort of battalion. Most of us have kids in the EAGLE thing. It's noticeable when those classes come out because they're such a small part of the school's population. Ten percent maybe. Almost everyone else in the school is Southeast Asian. Little Bangladesh, people call our neighborhood sometimes. Or Little Pakistan. Not the people who live here though.

■ ■ ■ ■

Sylvia calls to tell me she's losing heart. "These people," she says. At one house in the hills, the kids had piñatas full of candy in their rooms just for the hell of it.

Later, I look through her old letters. It's true. She is. In the beginning, she answered questions like this.

Q: Why do humans like applause?

A: I suspect it is because we are at a disadvantage compared with much of the animal kingdom. We lack sharp teeth or

101

claws. We are not the biggest or the fastest. And we evolved in an environment where we lived nomadically and were exposed daily to the terrifying forces of nature. Accordingly, we banded together in tight-knit groups to better protect ourselves. We built fires and told stories to make the dark nights pass by. Applause may be a way for us to make our weak hands sound thunderous.

By the end, it was like this.

Q: How did we end up here?

A: *We can, if need be, ransack the whole globe, penetrate into the bowels of the earth, descend to the bottom of the deep, travel to the farthest regions of this world, to acquire wealth, to increase our knowledge, or even only to please our eye and fancy.*

(William Derham, 1711)

■ ■ ■ ■

"How do you sleep at night knowing all this?"

"I've known it for a long, long time," she says.

It affects her in other ways, I think. Sylvia always wants to go see things, some nearby, some far away. The requirement is that they are disappearing faster than expected. The going, going, gone trips, I call them. She picks me up early, then we drive and drive until we reach the designated place. Then we walk around and look at things and I try to feel what she does. Once I took Eli. We stood and looked at some kind of meadow-land. He waited patiently until we could go back to the car.

Children cannot abide a vista, Sylvia said.

■ ■ ■ ■

There are little signs everywhere in the

library now that say BREATHE! BREATHE! How did everyone get so good at this breathing thing? I feel like it all happened while I was away.

Also, why has my mother sent me this box of old papers? She sent some to Henry too. Catherine went through them and promptly sent this to me. It's from high school, when my brother tried, inexplicably, to join the model UN club.

During the preparation for this trip, Henry was surely one of the most disappointing students I have dealt with in the field trip situation. When shown his duties, his apparent reaction was incredulity proceeded by levity. Also subject to discussion was his lack of thoughtfulness in letting others do his work.

Toward the end of the trip, however, he began to show an awareness and sensitivity to this impression and began to do his job seriously and enthusiastically. He was able to overcome his preoccupation with self and to participate in the duties and pleasures of the trip. If he can become more sensitive to other people's needs, he will be a welcomed addition to any group.

■ ■ ■ ■

I don't know what's wrong with me. I can't seem to stop making bad decisions. The weird thing is they don't sneak up on me. I can see them coming all the way down the pike.

My main bad decision is spending too much time traveling or being a fake shrink while ignoring the people I live with. Lately, it's my mother whom I'm on the phone with every evening. *Lizzie,* she says when she calls. *Lizzie, can you spare a minute?*

Everything is about the new baby. She is excited to come when she is born, but fears she is not really wanted, that they have asked her to visit only out of politeness. I don't know if this is true. My mother can be very good at helping out when help is needed. Once she gave away our Thanks-

105

giving turkey in the parking lot because she spied a needier family. "Come," I tell my mother. "Everyone is looking forward to it."

By the time I get off the phone, everybody's pissed. Eli wanted me to play War with him and has flung the cards all over his bed. Ben was going to show me this new game he made about *The Odyssey.*

I'm too tired for any of it. The compromise is that we all eat ice cream and watch videos of goats screaming like women.

■ ■ ■ ■

Even more mail than usual. I'm really hoping all these people who write to Sylvia are crazy, not depressed.

Some Jews saw walls being built around the ghetto and thought they still had time. Don't be fooled by everyone else's calm. Get out even when nobody is even considering it yet. When you look at 2060, southern Argentina might be a good place for your children since it's close to the Antarctic peninsula, the place where the survivor colonies will be built.

■ ■ ■ ■

This morning I was forced to learn about something called "climate departure," and later, at bedtime, when he was half asleep, I was forced to tell Ben about it. I only believe in math, he mumbled. Show me the math, okay?

But you don't want to look at the math again; you're never going back to that website where you put in the year Eli was born and then watched the numbers go up, up, up. No. Never.

"What's new with you guys?"
"Lizzie's become a crazy doomer."

In 1934, Churchill gave a speech to the Commons, attempting to describe the ruinous effects an air raid would have on the city of London. He was hoping such images of devastation would force even the most optimistic among them to consider what would happen if bombs rained down from the sky. The details were provided to him, he said, *by persons who are acquainted with the science.*

■ ■ ■ ■

Someone has put spikes on the fence around the playground. Not here, not here, not there either is the message to the pigeons. Feathered rats, the planners probably called them.

Catherine and I make small talk about the neighborhood. What's closing, what's opening. Are the Pakistani restaurants taking over the Indian ones? Are the Orthodox finally renting to the Tibetans? There's a new place that is half guitar shop, half bar. "Where did all these hipsters come from?" says my brother in his fleece-lined trucker's jacket.

There's a hopped-up guy inside the bodega saying, "I got lots and lots and lots and lots." Mohan turns to him. "My brother, tell me, what do you need?"

Last week, we ran into Amira and her mother here. Her name is Na'ila. I invited them over for tea and they came the next day along with her two older sisters. The sisters sat in a row on the couch and politely answered the questions I addressed to them all.

How is it different from where you used to live? We never had milk in a bottle before.

Amira and Eli played quietly at their feet. The Legos weren't working, so he went for the plastic ice cream. She seemed delighted by it. Later, when they were leaving, she touched my arm delicately. Until we meet again, she said, in the manner of someone who learned English from television.

■ ■ ■ ■

Catherine's birth plan keeps getting longer and longer. There are so many things on it. One of them is *Eye pillow (organic lavender)*. Henry told me last night he needs to get one ASAP.

I tell him to go to that hippie store on Seventh Avenue. Once as a joke, we went in there together. We held up quartz crystals, jingled tiny bells, flipped through some hemp clothing. The salesperson came over and asked if we were interested in energy healing. I don't really believe in it, my brother told her. She looked surprised. Why not? she said. You believe in the wind, don't you?

I'm not sure why, but all the women who fall for Henry are a weird mix of hard-edged and hippie-minded. The one before Catherine still sends him invoices for their cat's vet bills. *Blessings, blessings, blessings,* she signs them.

I go into the living room and turn the air

conditioner on full blast. Ben thinks it's wasteful to run it so high. What if we overload the grid? But I am hot and over-rule this. I kneel down so I can put my face right in front of it. Once sadness was considered one of the deadly sins, but this was later changed to sloth. (Two strikes then.)

■ ■ ■ ■

Henry and I make plans to meet for coffee at the place on his block. It is hard for him to get even that far away. "I'm on house arrest," he whispers. "I'm jumping out of my skin." I wish I could give him something for his nerves, but of course, I can't. I remind myself (as I often do) never to become so addicted to drugs or alcohol that I'm not allowed to use them.

So okay, no Klonopin. A walk in the park maybe. But the forecast tomorrow is for rain. Heavy winds too.

Oh, wait, they're already here. The dog

111

barks at the window, then at the recycling bin that has moved mysteriously. The news blares in from the living room. He wants to build a wall. It will have a beautiful door, he says.

Q: What are the best ways to prepare my children for the coming chaos?

A: You can teach them to sew, to farm, to build. Techniques for calming a fearful mind might be the most useful though.

My brother arrives at the diner with four shopping bags in hand. There's one of those things you nurse on, bottled water, energy bars, a humidifier, a gray sweater, and yes, yes, a lavender eye pillow. "Jesus," he says. "I've been out for hours. Are the nurses even going to let us take this all in?"

I'm torn because no, they are not, but I want to make sure he knows how impressed I am by his diligence. It seems like a good sign that my brother is keeping up with such things. I manage to get some approximation of this across.

We order coffee, cake, more cake. Henry finishes his and mine too. I ask what she's been feeding him. He waves away the question. Catherine's plan is to take a month off then go back to work. Her mother is coming for a week, then our mother, then it is just Henry. There's a smear of frosting on his chin. I point it out, give him a napkin.

The waitress comes to clear our plates. She puts down the bill in front of him, and even though he's richer now he passes it right to me. I give her the card that might have money on it. The waitress brings the slip back and I sign it. Henry leaves the tip.

I take the car service home. The sky is radiant. "I used to be a paperboy," Mr. Jimmy says.

■ ■ ■ ■

My husband is reading the Stoics before

breakfast. That can't be good, can it? Last night, I made him promise not to do that exercise on us. The one where you look down upon the person you love while he or she is sleeping and remind yourself: *Tomorrow you will die.*

He said okay. Why would he anyway? Didn't we already decide he would go first? He's in one of his cheerful moods. Perhaps because he's viewing this scene as if from a great height.

■ ■ ■ ■

There are fewer and fewer birds these days. This is the hole I tumbled down an hour ago. I finally stop clicking when my mother calls. She wants to tell me things are getting worse where she lives. Someone left bags of candy in all the white people's mailboxes. The note attached said, *Are there troubles in your neighborhood?*

■ ■ ■ ■

And Henry's started sending messages in code. *Heavy winds over here,* he writes, and it takes me a while to get it. Poor Catherine. The baby is due soon and she is going crazy on bed rest.

When I come over with some groceries, Henry hightails it out of there before I even take off my shoes. *You're just smoking, right?* I text from the bathroom. *No pills or powders,* he says.

Their apartment is messier than I've ever seen it. I heat up some soup for Catherine. Her hair is greasy and she's been sleeping in her mascara. I feel a surge of fondness for her. "This will be over soon, right?" "Right," I say. She holds the bowl in her lap without eating any. She is watching a man on YouTube who is dressed like a doctor.

I remember how it was at the end. The doctor said to make sure the baby kicked at least every four hours. If not, I was to come in. One morning the kicking stopped. It was the second day of a blizzard. *Stay off the roads,* the radio said. But the taxi driver sped through the icy streets for us. He told us about his wife and his four children back in Ghana. *Trust me,* he said. *We are almost there.*

■ ■ ■ ■

Today, I spotted Nicola outside the drugstore, but before I could react, she slipped inside. Later, it occurred to me. There's no way I could have kept from running into her all these years by chance alone.

Oh god, Eli's mother! The sanctimonious one who wants to make sure you know she went to a state school and her car's headlight is duct-taped in!

So she must be dodging me too.

■ ■ ■ ■

Mostly the people who take this meditation

116

class just want to know if they should be vegetarians or, if they already are, how to convert others. Margot is not interested in this debate. A tomato is just as alive as a cow, isn't it?

She is younger than I am, I think, but her hair has gone completely gray. I complimented her on it once. It happened the year I was widowed, she said.

■ ■ ■ ■

The due date is almost here and Henry is texting me every hour he is awake. I send him little things to distract him, like this article I read about how the superrich are buying doomsteads in New Zealand. There was a surge of interest after that report came out saying that the world's eight richest men have the same wealth as half of humanity combined.

The pros of New Zealand are that it's beautiful, politically stable, and moderate in climate. The cons are the government has restrictions about what you can name your kid. Sex Fruit and Fat Boy are forbidden. Violence and Number 16 Bus Shelter are okay.

I'm going to name the baby Fat Sex Bus, he tells me.

■ ■ ■ ■

The last supper. We are served a boring, vitamin-filled meal that befits the expecting parents to be. I ask Catherine if she is scared. "Sometimes," she says. "Sometimes a little." The baby is due in two days, a girl, but they are keeping the name a secret. We spend a while trying to guess it.
Anna?
Emma?
Ella?
Lily?
"You're getting warm," she says.

It's the night of the back-to-school concert. Before we can walk into the auditorium, we have to show our IDs and the ticket his teacher sent us last week. On the corner of the ticket there is a number that shows how many people are in your family. There is a warning not to bring any extra guests to the performance because SAFETY FIRST!

Eli stands in the front row of the bleachers next to Amira. He is wearing his lucky pants and his lucky shirt, but he looks nervous. The last song is his favorite one, he has told me. I can see him gathering confidence as they move through the other, lesser numbers. Then all at once the kids close their eyes and begin to sway. Everyone leans forward, trying to see. They sing that their lives are like a drop of water, no more, in an endless sea. Whatever they make will not stand; it will crumble to the ground before their very eyes. And all the money in the world could not buy them a moment more.

Nothing lasts forever is the conclusion reached. An exception is made for the earth and the sky.

The baby is here! She arrived last night at 3:04 a.m. Her name is Iris and everyone thinks it's a good name.

They got a private room, thank God, but Catherine is still wild-eyed. Nothing went according to plan. There was no calming music, no birthing ball, no soft socks, no warm compresses. They gave her an enema, an epidural, and Pitocin. The baby came so fast that Catherine's doctor didn't make it there in time. She arrived an hour late, dressed for an evening out, and delivered the placenta.

All this I get in whispers from Henry. "There was so much blood! They were mopping it up with towels! You wouldn't believe it, Lizzie," he says.

But I would. I had a baby in this shitty hospital too. There's that *ding, ding, ding* as you go down the hallways, all those machines conducting their business. Even the buzzing of these awful lights is stored somewhere deep in my body. As soon as I walked through the door, it rose to the surface.

■ ■ ■ ■

On the last night that she's in town, my mother comes over for dinner. She has been helping Henry and Catherine with the baby. She is thrilled by all the hard work. She says she can't remember the last time Henry paid so much attention to her. She talks about the goodness of God. She cooks us spaghetti carbonara.

Later, she plays an endless game of War with Eli and expresses concern about how closely Ben follows the political news. "You should pace yourself," she tells him. "We're only about twenty minutes into this."

In the morning, I drive her to the airport. She is sorry to go. "Don't you think I could be more helpful if I lived here?" I don't know what to say. Yes, of course, but she lives on a fixed income, has no savings. Where could she afford to live? She gives me a tentative smile. "I don't take up much space." I squeeze her hand, then turn on the radio. I flip until I find an easy listening station. But then I realize it's God radio. A question is posed to us.

The critical question for our generation — and for every generation — is this: If you could have heaven, with no sickness, and with all the friends you ever had on earth, and all the food you ever liked, and all the leisure activities you ever enjoyed, and all the natural beauties you ever saw, all the physical pleasures you ever tasted, and no human conflict or any natural disasters, could you be satisfied with heaven, if Christ was not there?

Yup.

I kiss her goodbye, make her promise to call me later. She insisted I not go to short-term parking, just drop her at the curb, but from my rearview mirror I see my mistake as she struggles through the revolving door. Ten minutes after I drop her off, Henry texts me. *The mothers are gone! The mothers are gone! When are you coming over?*

■ ■ ■ ■

I spend a morning trying to find my old nursing pump for Catherine. Here it is, finally, in the back of a closet. Odd to see it again. I remember the weekend I weaned Eli, I drove up to visit an old friend, one of the few left who is married without children. She and her husband live in an old Victorian house and everything in it is carefully chosen and beautiful. She made me a fancy dinner — rack of lamb, mint jelly, chocolate soufflé — and I tried to act like a human being, not like someone on the lam from her kid.

But then in the middle of the night the milk started coming in, and my shirt got so wet that I sat on the toilet and squeezed it into a towel, worrying about what to say, where to put it, would it smell sour?

I was up most of the night. My body hurt;

my brain did too. I thought I might hide the towel under the bed or pack it in with my things to get rid of at home. I couldn't tell which plan was best, but in the morning when I saw my friend, I said, That beautiful towel you gave me, I've ruined it, so sorry, I can pay you for it, and driving home alone, radio on, everything was so green — you wouldn't believe how green it was — and alongside the road there were flowers and vegetables, but no one there minding the stand, just a box to leave money in, and even that not locked.

I should have taken it.

■ ■ ■ ■

I get a series of ecstatic texts from a newly divorced friend who has met someone. "I can only imagine what it would be like to be this age and then suddenly fall in love," I tell Ben. "You are in love," he corrects me.

Later, he runs his hand along my leg in the dark then stops. "Are you wearing my long johns?" "I was cold," I tell him. We make up a proverb (*Married sex is like taking off your own pants*), fool around, go to sleep happy.

■ ■ ■ ■

Hippie test, courtesy of a book Sylvia gave me. I'm hoping there's some kind of extra credit or else I really bombed it.

Where You At?

Trace the water you drink from precipitation to tap. How many days till the moon is full? . . . From what direction do winter storms generally come in your region? Name five grasses in your area. Name five resident and five migratory birds . . . Were the stars out last night?

From where you are reading this, point north.

For some reason, where I am at is in front of this mirror, pressing my gums to see if they'll bleed again. No. Good. I should get back to work, but instead I stand there making faces until someone comes in. It's the blond girl with the bitten nails. She used to do a lot of crank, I remember. She had this story about how she was in a bathroom the first time it hit. The buzz of the party grew louder and louder, and she thought she'd return to find locusts had descended.

■ ■ ■ ■

I had that thought again. The one with numbers in it. It bent the light.

Eli is at the kitchen table, trying all his markers one by one to see which still work. Ben brings him a bowl of water so he can dip them in to test. According to the current trajectory, New York City will begin to

experience dramatic, life-altering tempera-
tures by 2047.

■ ■ ■ ■

My friend who works in hospice says don't
tell dying people they won't be around for
the beach trip, apples in fall, etc. No more
do that than knock a crutch out from under
a person with a broken leg.

No more apples soon; apples need frost.

I decide to reshelve by the big window. It's
beautiful out. There's a group of students
with linked arms, chanting something in the
quad. I follow a trail of candy wrappers that
are lined up along the sill. The top of that
tree is on fire. Or else it's fall again.

■ ■ ■ ■

"Did you look at the river, Lizzie?" Sylvia

asks me when she picks me up from the train. I lie and say yes. It pains her the way everyone goes around with their heads down these days.

The leaves are nearly gone. We pass one apple orchard then another. "People only want the perfect ones," she says, "especially when they pick them themselves, so all the bruised or split or wormy ones get left on the ground for the deer." There are thousands and thousands of deer here. Soon it will be hunting season. "At least most people who hunt up here hunt for food, not sport," she says. I watch them bound away as we turn down her dirt road. "Why don't they farm deer?" I wonder. "Is it because they are too pretty?" She shakes her head. "It's because they panic when penned."

On the way home, the train stops for a long time outside the city. I look at the trees along the river. There are still a few leaves on them. Some people at the water's edge. But hasn't the world always been going to hell in a handbasket? I asked her. Parts of the world, yes, but not the world entire, she said.

It's pouring when I come out of the subway station. There's a low hum in my head. "Boohoo," says the friendly-looking white man who passes me on the street. "Boohoo!"

Am I crying?

I pass by the bodega. "We have garlic now," Mohan calls out to me. I pay with pennies, but he is nice about it. "Pennies are money too," he says.

There is a miniature American flag by the register now, right beside the postcard of Ganesh. But Mohan is not worried. "Even if this man wins, he will not stay," he tells me. "Now he has money, planes, beautiful things. He is a bird. Why be a bird in a cage?"

■ ■ ■ ■

THREE

■ ■ ■ ■

After the election, Ben makes many small wooden things. One to organize our utensils, one to keep the trash can from wobbling. He spends hours on them. "There, I fixed it," he says.

A turtle was mugged by a gang of snails. The police came to take a report, but he couldn't help them. "It all happened so fast," he said.

And in the ether, people asking the same question again and again. To the yours-to-losers, to the both-the-samers, to the wreck-it-allers.

Happy now?

The path is getting . . . narrower. That's how Ben told me. He was doing the math in his head.

But it could still . . . ?
It's not impossible.

And so we stayed up and watched until the end.

At school, Eli's friend boasts that he will kill the president using a lightsaber. Then he says no, a throwing star is better. My son comes home upset. His friend is going about things the wrong way, he thinks. "What is the right way?" I ask him.

Dig a trap, cover it with leaves.

There is advice everywhere, some grand, some practical. The practical advice spreads quickly and creates consequences.

Women of reproductive age are being urged

to get IUDs. They can last six to twelve years and so might outlast the shuttering of the clinics. But it's suddenly hard to get in to see a doctor; the appointments are all booked for months and the waiting rooms at the walk-in clinics are full of nervous white women.

Q: Do angels need sleep?

A: It is unlikely, though we cannot be completely sure.

"Should we get a gun?" Ben asks. But it's America. You don't even get on the news if you shoot less than three people. I mean, isn't that the last right they'll take away? He looks at me. His grandfather's last name was twice as long as his. They shortened it at Ellis Island.

It was the same after 9/11, there was that hum in the air. Everyone everywhere talking about the same thing. In stores, in restaurants, on the subway. My friend met me at the diner for coffee. His family fled Iran one week before the Shah fell. He didn't want to talk about the hum. I pressed him though. Your people have finally fallen into history, he said. The rest of us are already here.

■ ■ ■ ■

Everything is better in the quiet car. In the quiet car, everyone is calm. Ben presses his leg against mine. We read side by side as Eli builds many-roomed mansions. A person across the aisle who is chatting with his friend in Spanish is asked to leave by the conductor. "Right now?" he says. "While the train is moving?"

In the hotel room, there are many hotel channels, but all disappoint.

■ ■ ■ ■

We go to the Smithsonian. They want to see the space stuff. I want to see the hominids. In the afternoon, we tour the monuments, speak solemnly about democracy. Coming to D.C. was Ben's idea. It's creepier than I imagined to be here. Soon, soon, soon, is the loop in my head. Ben has this plan to spend the next few months visiting historical things with Eli. I want to lay a foundation, he told me, but for what exactly he doesn't say.

Our very last stop is the Spy Museum. Ben grumbles because I seem to have picked the only museum in the city that is not free. He says he'll wait in the lobby. I'm happy though because we narrowly missed having to go to the Holocaust Museum.

Eli is excited about this place. We are given a cover story, must memorize it quickly, then answer a series of questions. There is a hidden passageway that kids can crawl through. I limp around, looking at the exhibits. There are lipstick guns. Camera guns.

But the best thing is an ordinary-looking pair of glasses. Cyanide tipped. To be used if you are caught by the enemy so you don't betray anyone.

■ ■ ■ ■

It's going to be too much, Sylvia said. People who do this kind of work will break down, people will get sick and die. I remember what she said when I called her the day after. *Up in smoke! Up in smoke!*

She predicted all of this before it happened. In chaotic times, people long for a strongman, she said. But I didn't believe her. Hardly anyone did.

But now there's a woman in the bathroom and there's shit all over the floor. I hand paper towels under the door. Expensive-looking boots, I note. We don't speak and later I am careful not to look at the shoes of anyone.

At the circulation desk, Lorraine is being shown the X-rays again. Patiently, she nods her head. She used to sing in a club, someone told me. She has grown children and a husband who is dying of some slow, awful thing. I don't get into people's business, she told me once. The only piece of advice she's ever given me was: *Take care of your teeth.*

But later, I see her in the break room yelling at our coworker. "You are a child! You have acted like a child!" she tells the one who decided not to vote.

Ben's sister told him there is a sign now on the door of the fancy grocery store in her town. NO POLITICS, PLEASE, it reads.

Q: How can I tell if those around me would become good Germans?

A: There is a historian named Timothy Snyder who has studied in great detail how past societies have descended into fascism. In his book *On Tyranny,* he made the following suggestions:

Make eye contact and small talk. This is not just polite. It is a way to stay in touch with your surroundings, break down unnecessary social barriers, and come to understand whom you should and should not trust. If we enter a culture of denunciation, you will want to know the psychological landscape of your daily life.

My book-ordering history is definitely going to get me flagged by some evil government algorithm. Lots and lots of books about Vichy France and the French Resistance and more books than any civilian could possibly need about spy craft and fascism. Luckily, there is a Jean Rhys novel in there and a book for Eli called *How to Draw Robots.* That'll throw them off the scent.

There is a period after every disaster in which people wander around trying to figure out if it is truly a disaster. Disaster psychologists use the term "milling" to describe most people's default actions when they find themselves in a frightening new situation.

That's the name for what we're doing, Sylvia says.

■ ■ ■ ■

140

"Get everything done now," Ben insists. He is worried one or both of us will lose our jobs. But I don't like to go to the dentist. Won't he just have bad news for me? "Please, Lizzie," he says. "You've had that temporary crown for years."

A woman walks into a dentist's office and says, "I think I'm a moth."
The dentist tells her, "You shouldn't be here. You should be seeing a psychiatrist . . ."
The woman replies, "I am seeing a psychiatrist."
The dentist says, "Then what are you doing here?"
And she says, "Your light was on."

■ ■ ■ ■

Henry's always calling me for advice too, cajoling me to come over. And when I do he hands the baby to me and lies down on the couch and stares at the ceiling. He lets everything go to hell all day, then does a mad rush to get everything together before Catherine gets home at seven. I've been treading lightly, but he seems worse, not better. Luckily, Iris is an easy baby. It's Henry who seems ready to burst into tears.

Ben isn't much better. He turns the volume off so he never hears his voice, but sometimes I listen. Now he is talking about something in space. The moon maybe. How we should go there again. I woke up in the middle of the night last night. The dog was barking, or maybe it was just in my dream. Today NASA found seven new Earth-size planets. So there's that.

■ ■ ■ ■

The sky is dull, a soft feathery gray, streaked here and there with clouds. Well, yes, I would, sir. I would like to hear the GOOD NEWS. I will read this pamphlet forthwith!

■ ■ ■ ■

Ben looks into the Israel thing; I look into

142

the idea of true north.

"The problem is it's matrilineal," he says. "I mean, you guys would have to convert."

"I don't want to live in Israel. That's even worse."

"I know," he says. "You're right."

I think about those people shouting, Blood and soil! Blood and soil!

"But let's keep it in our pocket," I tell him.

Now when I see my neighbors the voice in my head gets all Jesusy. One of you will betray me. But which? Is it you Mrs. Kovinski?

■ ■ ■ ■

Take care of your teeth, take care of your teeth, take care of your teeth, my monkey mind says. The class is thinning out again. This morning Margot talked about the difference between falling and floating. With practice, she says, one may learn to accept the feeling of groundlessness without existential fear. This is akin to the way an experienced parachutist or astronaut might enjoy the wide view from above even as he hurtles through space.

She gave us a formula: suffering = pain + resistance.

■ ■ ■ ■

Today Mr. Jimmy starts up a conversation with me as soon as I get in. I'm so tired I hardly listen to him, just nod here and there. Now he's going on about background checks again. "I check all my drivers. I mean, when I had other drivers I did. You have to be careful." I nod, sure, sure. "Otherwise you could just have some Mohammed come in, get a car to drive, fill it up with explosives . . ."

He pulls up to my building. I fumble with my purse as he smiles at me, telling me to take my time. The car smells like fake trees. "I'm a little short today, sorry," I tell him. "No problem," he says, and waves his hand magnanimously.

144

And just like that I'm free.

■ ■ ■ ■

It used to be simple to put up flyers at the library, but now they're all in a glass case. There's a key to open it and people have to ask us for it at the desk. My boss did that after someone started putting up hateful screeds.

There is a theory that new hate has been unleashed. Another that the amount of hate is exactly the same as it's always been. Lorraine subscribes to the latter one. The only difference is that more people are noticing it, she says.

Someone returns a book called *The Sayings of the Desert Fathers.* I flip through it while I eat my lunch.

A time is coming when men will go mad, and when they see someone who is not mad, they will attack him, saying, "You are mad, you are not like us."

■ ■ ■ ■

Henry keeps sterilizing the bottles then resterilizing them. I want to explain to him that it's overkill, but my guess is he's following strict directives. I hold Iris and play with her for a while, then put her smack in the middle of their king-size bed and go to the kitchen to see what's keeping him. He's sterilizing the metal tongs that he uses to put the plastic bottles in the boiling water. It's cool in the apartment, but he's sweating buckets.

"Why don't you take a nap?" I say. "I'll watch her." He whirls around to look at me. "Where is she?" I tell him I put her in the middle of the bed. He drops the tongs to go in there. She is fast asleep. "She could have fallen off," he says. "Henry, she can't even roll over yet." His hands are shaking. "She could have gotten hurt," he insists.

I make him lie down on the couch, put a

blanket on him. Thirty seconds of protest and he's out. He's not doing well with this sleep deprivation. There's a reason it's used as a tool of torture. But still, everyone I know is trying to sleep less. Insomnia as a badge of honor. Proof that you are paying attention.

■ ■ ■ ■

There was a bomb threat yesterday at Eli's school. And there are rumors that a woman had her hijab pulled off on Coney Island Avenue. All the EAGLE mothers cluster together before pickup to discuss the situation. "For starters, they need to stop calling this area Little Pakistan," one says.

When I get to work, I look up some articles on Disaster Psychology in hopes of better assisting all the people wandering around here lately.

Much of the population was in a mild stupor, depressed, congregating in small unstable groups, and prone to rumors of doom.

But I don't know. That's pretty much every day here.

■ ■ ■ ■

Margot's class is too crowded lately so I've been skipping it. "Are you sure that's the best chant for you?" Ben asks me. He must have heard me in the shower.

Sentient creatures are numberless. I vow to save them.

Now I'm rummaging around in a drawer, trying to find some pants that fit. These new dryers are too hot. Most of our clothes shrank before I realized it. Ben still wears these shirts that are too short at the sleeves, that strain at the buttons. He's got that old ancestral guilt. Maybe it's me, he said. Maybe I got too big.

■ ■ ■ ■

When I arrive, Henry is standing in the
doorway with his coat on, keys in hand. I
give him a hug. "The baby's asleep," he
says. "I'm going to go get some groceries." I
go in to look at her. Yes, she is sleeping the
right way. I turn on their computer. YouTube
videos about babyproofing your house. She
can't even crawl, people!

I can't even believe I'm here before work. I
need to put my foot down, that's what
everybody says. We are in his kitchen. That
clever devil Catherine went to work at six
a.m. to get a head start on her meeting prep.

"Do you ever think it's weird that we even
have families?" Henry says.

I take Iris out in her stroller. It is a misty
gray morning. I pull the plastic down over
her. The Buddha once described how his
father protected him from the elements.

149

A white sunshade was held over me day and night so that no cold or heat or dust or grit or dew might inconvenience me.

(Onward we go, inconvenienced by dew!)

■ ■ ■ ■

When I get home, there's a postcard from Sylvia. On the front, a spindly tree surrounded by a wire fence. "Miracle Tree" is the caption. She's at a conference about Fukushima. I said I couldn't go, that I had to watch the baby.

I will caution you against choosing Japan as your next foreign travel destination unless you enjoy strict behavior rules, massive industrial skyscrapers, and paying ten dollars for a weird pastry and coffee in a can. If these things entice you, then hurry right over, my friend, you can't even laugh loudly here in public without drawing a stare, and Tokyo is hell on earth.

On the way back, she meets me in the city

for dinner. I tell her that I've been thinking that we should buy some land somewhere colder. That if climate departure happens in New York when predicted, Eli and Iris could —

"Do you really think you can protect them? In 2047?" Sylvia asks. I look at her. Because until this moment, I did, I did somehow think this. She orders another drink. "Then become rich, very, very rich," she says in a tight voice.

■ ■ ■ ■

Henry wants to confess something. We walk a long circle around the neighborhood before he manages it. He says he's having bad thoughts about the baby, that he keeps imagining terrible things. It's normal, I assure him. I tell him how I used to worry all the time that Eli would choke on a grape. "No, not like that, Lizzie," he says. "It's not her. It's me."

Later, I keep thinking about those people

you read about in the paper, the ones who are discovered by animal protection services. They live in a studio apartment, go to work every day — their neighbors don't notice a thing — but when they break down the door, there's an alligator or a boa constrictor in there. Something that could kill them.

FOUR

It's afternoon, but the sky is already dark with rain. We wait on the platform for the express. The old man beside us starts to cough violently. Henry freezes. To a man with a hammer . . .

■ ■ ■ ■

Is it the amount or the frequency of these thoughts that causes concern?
Do these thoughts cause marked distress?
Do these thoughts significantly interfere with your normal routine?

■ ■ ■ ■

"You can't tell anyone this," he says. "Lizzie, you have to promise." I feel like he is tying me up with rope. "I'm bad at secrets, you know that." He shakes his head. "Not when it counts."

He won't even bathe her. He's washing her with a squirt gun now.
Lizzie, what's going on? Lizzie, what's going on?
Repeat ten times.
So yeah, I tell Ben.

■ ■ ■ ■

There is a tradition in Judaism that happiness and sorrow must be intermingled. On Passover, you are instructed to remove drops of wine before drinking it to lessen your pleasure. Each drop removed represents a tragedy that befell those who went before you.

It's the same at weddings. The couple breaks a glass by stepping on it together.

156

This is so they will remember past sorrows in the midst of their present joy.

Sometimes I think my family just brought a pile of broken glass to Ben's doorstep. He's been quiet since I told him about everything. Well, not quite everything. There was one thing I left out. I think Henry's stopped going to meetings. He told me he goes, but I waited outside the other day and I didn't see him.

"This can't go on forever," Ben says. "Just give me time to stabilize him," I tell him. He nods, looks away.

The pieces of glass from a wedding were meant to be saved. If the husband died first, the wife prepared his body for burial by weighting his eyelids with the shards. If the wife died first, it was the husband's job to do this. I wish I had known this. I wish I had kept those shards.

■ ■ ■ ■

Sylvia quit the foundation last week; there's no hope anymore, only witness, she thinks. She tells me that she feels like she is in a car, trying to accelerate. Some people she works with are trying to get in the car. Some are throwing themselves in front of it to prevent her from leaving.

She's started forwarding me jokes.

The leaders of Russia, Syria, and America are arguing about who is the best at catching criminals. The secretary-general of the UN decides to give them a test. He releases a rabbit into a forest and tells them they must catch it.

The American team goes in. They place animal informants throughout the forest. They question all plant and mineral witnesses. After three months of extensive investigations, they conclude that rabbits do not exist.

The Syrian team goes in. After two weeks with no leads, they burn down the forest, killing everything in it, including the rabbit. The rabbit was a dangerous rebel, they report.

The Russian team goes in last. They come out two hours later with a badly beaten bear. The bear is yelling, "Okay! Okay! I'm a rabbit! I'm a rabbit!"

■ ■ ■ ■

Eli asks if he can look up something about robots. I hand him my computer and go to the kitchen to make him some macaroni and cheese. When I come back, he is watching a video from a British morning show. It's about a robot named Samantha. She is made to look like a human and has two settings, the inventor says. In sex mode, she can moan if you touch her breasts. In family mode, she can tell jokes or talk about philosophy.

■ ■ ■ ■

Tonight it takes four stories before I can get him to bed. The one that does the trick is about a dog who is on his way to a dog party being held at the top of a tree. On his way there, he meets other dogs headed to the festivities. They stop to talk.
Do you like my hat?
I do not.
Good-by!
Good-by!

This is my dream of how neighbors should talk to each other.

Instead, it's Mrs. Kovinski knocking at seven a.m. "I see you've got your poison paper," she says. She's picked up the Sunday *Times* from the hallway, brought it to my door.

■ ■ ■ ■

All day, Ben lies on the couch, reading a giant history of war. But he got it at a used-book store so it only goes up to World War I.

In the summer of 1914, there was an electric tension in the air. It would not be long until the descent into the madness of the first fully mechanized war. The British statesman Sir Edward Grey famously predicted what was to come. "The lamps are going out all over Europe; we shall not see them lit again in our lifetime."

At bedtime, Eli and I start *Prince Caspian.* At the beginning, the children are pulled out of a train station and land on an uninhabited island. They wander around until they find a bit of a stone wall. Eli realizes it is the ruins of the Narnia castle before I do. Then he starts asking questions. Will he still be alive when I die? If not, what will he do?

I tell him that old dodge. That it will be a long, long time before I do. That we will all live a long, long time.

But this is not what he wants to know.

■ ■ ■ ■

Lately, Ben has been sending up trial balloons about other neighborhoods. But when we look up the rents they are ridiculously high. I keep worrying he will suggest New Jersey, but he never does.

He has an idea for the summer though. He wants to send Eli to camp at a historic estate where they teach kids to churn butter and herd goats. Eli does not want to go. "It's you that wants to go," I tell him.

■ ■ ■ ■

I keep wondering how we might channel all of this dread into action. One night Ben and I go to a meeting about justice at the Unitarian church down the street. Good people all around, making plans, assisting — so why do I feel so embarrassed?

Most are older than we are; they speak of how others have helped them; they give thanks for those who have reached out and call on us to think about the less fortunate.

It's church. I remember now how it went.

"I thought you wanted community," Ben says afterward. But not so much. Not like that. All that eye contact. "Not my tribe," I tell him.

Q: How does a Unitarian walk on water?

A: She waits until winter.

I miss the express bus and have to take the local home instead. Just the other day I heard one woman tell another that slowness is a form of goodness. This bus is full of old Russian people holding shopping bags between their feet. I sit across from a hot guy in a green coat who looks as if he's trying to place me. When I was younger, I sometimes knew why a man was staring at me, but these days it's often no more than a lapse in memory.

He has a pouch of tobacco in his pocket and a ratty backpack that looks like it's been to war. There's a book sticking out of it, but not far enough to read its title. Ben told me once that the Greeks had this term, *epoché,* meaning "I suspend judgment." Useful for those of us prone to making common cause with strangers on buses. Sudden alliances, my brother calls them. I have to be careful. My heart is prodigal.

It's raining. The bus is full. It's reached that density where being seated feels like a form of guilt. I look around. I will grudgingly stand for the infirm and the pregnant and those with children. But miraculously, it is all able-bodied teenagers with earbuds. I forgot my phone, or I too would have blotted out all these humans.

The guy in the green coat keeps glancing at me. "From the library," I tell him, and he nods slowly, respectfully, it seems. "Yes, yes, that's it," he says. He has a slight accent and I wonder if he comes from some distant country where librarians are held in high esteem.

We get off at Coney Island Avenue. When he stands up, I see it is a field guide to mushrooms. Pouring now. The pigeons have all flown away. The drug dealer from 5C holds the door open for me. We shake the rain off our umbrellas.

■ ■ ■ ■

Sylvia has a new escape plan. She wants to buy a trailer in the darkest place in America. She lived there once years ago with an ex who was an amateur astronomer. It's in Nevada somewhere, hours and hours from the nearest city. On a clear night, you can see the Pinwheel galaxy with the naked eye, she says. Later, I look it up and learn it is twenty-five million light-years away.

No more campaigning, no more fund-raising, no more obligatory notes of hope. Already things she worked on for years have been swept away with the stroke of a pen. All she wants now is to go somewhere quiet and dark, she says.

Withdrawal to the desert is called *anachoresis* in Greek.

■ ■ ■ ■

The meditation class is no longer crowded. I find out a lot of people left recently because of something Margot said. Someone asked her what she thought about the waves of recent allegations in the press. She said that it caused her great sadness to think of these men's dishonorable actions. But she dismissed the language of victims and perpetrators. When she was asked about punishment, she spoke instead of reincarnation. Everyone here has done everything to everyone else, she said.

Which explains why today it's just me and three straight guys listening to her. She is talking about how *dukkha,* which is usually translated as "suffering," can have other meanings. In Tibetan Buddhism, the word is sometimes slanted differently, she says. Instead of saying that life is suffering, they might say that life is tolerable. As in just barely.

■ ■ ■

Nowhere feels like home anymore. That's what my brother says as we walk around the park, his sleeping baby strapped to his chest.

"You have to see a real shrink," I tell him. "I don't think I'm a real one."

He's been on our couch for ten days now. He sees Iris when I arrange it. This because he got high and cheated on Catherine with an old girlfriend. Then he went home and confessed. There were a couple of weeks of back and forth, but then she kicked him out for good.

Two weeks and three couches later, Henry is back at our place. I remember now. My brother is a terrible roommate.

He paces endlessly around our apartment. It reminds me of those miserable weeks when he quit cold turkey. Something went wrong with his legs. He couldn't stop moving them. All night long, he would toss and turn. There was no position that was comfortable. My brain feels scraped, he said.

■ ■ ■ ■

Ben is being patient, but it's hard with my brother always here. It would be different if either one of them had an office. Henry's still doing the greeting cards, but I'm worried Catherine will have had enough of that too. I stay up late and try to help him brainstorm. We come up with a few ideas, but I don't say the first ones that pop into my head.

To a Brother Who Is a Burden . . .
To a Sister Who Never Made It Big . . .

■ ■ ■ ■

Henry is drinking all the milk. Henry is losing the remote. Henry is mad at Eli for

168

coming into the living room so early. Henry comes back late at night, forgets his key and has to be buzzed in. Henry says he never should have had a kid, it was his worst idea ever. Later, Eli says, "You wanted to have me, right?"

It's summer and there's nowhere for anyone to go.

"Why did you wash your hands for so long?"
"They were very dirty."

■ ■ ■ ■

Catherine has already served Henry with divorce papers. She is moving quickly in her usual way. Henry seems sad but mostly relieved. I told him he has to do something to get better, otherwise he might lose custody completely. Margot agreed to see him. Me too, though it's unorthodox.

It takes some doing, but I finally talk Henry

into meeting her. Afterward, we go back to my place. Eli is sitting alone by the window. "When I look at a tree or a bird, I can see the air around it," he announces. "He reminds me of me," Henry says. "Don't say that," I tell him, more sharply than I intend.

■ ■ ■ ■

I meant to call Sylvia back; I meant to, I did. But then Eli got the flu and I spent the night by his bed with a bucket. *Evacuate. Evacuate,* said our new talking alarm at four a.m. Ben and I fought about whose idea it was to get it.

What I mean to say is that it took me a week to get back to Sylvia. When I did all I got was a recording.

The number you have reached has been disconnected.

■ ■ ■ ■

In those disaster movies, if a person sees something from the time before, a phone charger, say, or the Statue of Liberty, she starts to weep.

■ ■ ■ ■

"You have to help me, Lizzie," my brother says. "I am," I tell him. "I am helping you." I sit him on the couch, put on *My Strange Addiction.*

Always a soothing hour of television. At least I don't eat talcum powder, one can comfort oneself. At least I'm not in love with the Verrazzano Bridge.

■ ■ ■ ■

Margot tells Henry that the worst thoughts must be spoken out loud. If they are held back, they will only grow more powerful. It reminds me of something my mother used to say — *Gods suppressed become devils.*

At the end of the second session, Margot gives us a workbook to take home with us. In the back of it are terrible exercises, none of which Henry will do.

But I did something stupid tonight, just before the end of my shift. I read an article about a person who received a face transplant, and now I know exactly what happens if you shoot yourself in the head when you are eighteen and somehow live.

The magazine warned me at the beginning that there would be disturbing pictures, but not how long they would disturb me or how I'd remember that Henry told me once a gun is best because you have to do the math just right with pills. And there was no warning at all about the words in the article, even though the caption to the picture was

The face serenely waits on the table for the surgeons.

■ ■ ■ ■

My brother never seems to sleep anymore. "You should join the military," I tell him. They've been studying the brain of the white-crowned sparrow to find out how it can fly for seven days without sleeping. The idea is to make it possible for soldiers to stay awake that long too. The Continuous Assisted Performance program, they call it.

Go to sleep, I used to tell him. I'll wake you up when we're somewhere.

■ ■ ■ ■

All afternoon, it's crazy hot. People are out on their stoops, talking and playing cards. An old man salutes me as we pass. Eli sidesteps some chicken bones and beer bottles on the way to the gumball machine. He gets a tiny rubber monster. This is the happiest day, he tells me.

But Henry is playing video games all night. He seems a little high, but I can't prove it. And he keeps trying to call Catherine, but he only ever gets her voice mail. The custody hearing is in two months. I just have to keep him alive until then, I joke to Ben. He doesn't laugh. I distract myself by staying up late, googling prepper things.

Start a Fire with Gum Wrapper and a Battery

Use the foil-backed wrapper to short-circuit an AA battery and create a flame. First, tear the wrapper into an hourglass shape and touch the foil to the positive and negative battery terminals. The electrical current will briefly cause the paper wrapper to ignite. Use the flame to light a candle or tinder.

What to Do If You Run Out of Candles

A can of tuna can provide hours of light. Stab a small hole in the top of an oil-packed tuna can, then roll a two-by-five-inch piece of newspaper into a wick. Shove the wick into the hole, leaving a half inch exposed. Wait a moment for the oil to soak to the top of the wick, then light with matches. Your new oil lamp will burn for almost two hours and the tuna will still be good to eat afterward.

* * *

Later, Ben comes into the living room, sees what I'm doing, and walks away. I follow him into our room. "You're weary of me, aren't you?" I say, and he says in the weariest voice imaginable, "No, I'm not. I just need to go to bed."

In the morning, he calls his sister. They talk for a long time. When he gets off, he tells me they are leaving on a three-week road trip to the California coast and we are invited. Glamping, she calls it. Do we want to go?

"I can't," I tell him. "I have to stay here."

Ben has that resigned look he gets these days when we talk about my brother. "Think about it," he says. "You have obligations to this family too, Lizzie."

But how can I leave him alone? Already,

175

I'm hiding my sleeping pills in a sock under my bed.

■ ■ ■ ■

Of course, Ben's worried I won't keep my head above water. Last time Henry was drowning, I dove in right after him. I left school and never went back again. Henry had stopped working. He wasn't seeing anyone. He just stayed in that apartment in Staten Island, high, until he ran out of drugs and had to go down the street to get some more.

I remember this one day I came and he was like a half-Henry, flickering in and out. You have to stop, I said, let me help you. It won't work, he said. It never works. You could go to meetings this time, I said. I might as well have signed him up for a trip to Mars. But then a few nights later he called me up giddy: he had an idea. He'd seen something on YouTube about the monks of Mount Athos. He made me watch it and call him right back. I could go there, he said. It's beautiful, there's nothing there.

They interviewed this one monk, middle-aged, American, a professor once. He had fled Boston, come there and never left. He showed the reporter where the ossuary was. All the skulls of the dead monks who had ever lived there, stacked up neatly like wood in a shed. He had no fear of death: I know where I'll end up, he said, and then an offhand wave toward them. He hadn't left the island since he was twenty-six and he wouldn't now, though his mother was dying. The reporter asked again: Even though your mother is dying? Even so, he said. His smile was so beautiful a chill went through me. No, I told Henry. I'd never see you again.

Tonight he's pacing back and forth, back and forth, across our tiny living room. "If anything happens to me, I'm leaving you Iris," he says. "Nothing is going to happen to you," I tell him. "Also, you can't."

Saturday and my plan is to do a bunch of errands. I'm at the supermarket before the doors are even open yet. It's just me and one other woman in a caftan. She looks focused. An extreme couponer possibly.

I've been watching this show about them. It's exactly like those shows about drug addicts minus the family ambush at the end. My favorite part is when the person comes up to the cashier with ten shopping carts. The total is always staggering, and there is a moment when it seems like the shopper might make a run for it. But then comes the music.

The person opens an enormous binder and starts handing the cashier coupon after coupon. With each one, the total ticks down.

How low can you go? How low can you go? *(The eternal question.)*

Someone says hello to me and I see it's the

hot guy from the bus. He is wearing running clothes, which lowers my opinion of him. "What are you up to?" he asks me. The manager looks out at us through the glass. The doors swing open. "Not much," I tell him. He pulls a nub of a cigarette out of his pocket, smokes it, then takes off running.

So okay, maybe not American.

Later, I take Eli to the new dollar store to get a plastic colander. He runs up and down the aisles ecstatically. "Who made all these things?" he asks me. "The Invisible Hand," I tell him.

■ ■ ■ ■

"I'm worried about you," Ben says. This because I said something I thought I only thought. Eli was hounding me about his cereal. Where was it? Why didn't I get it? Why couldn't I go back to the store? I hate everyone, I said.

Mildly, I'd argue, but not mildly enough apparently, because Eli burst into tears.

So now Ben announces that they are going to go on the trip with his sister. They are going whether I come or not. Three weeks. They've never been away that long. I repeat that I can't go and he packs them up in a weird, ominous silence.

But as soon as Ben gets to his sister's house, he calls me. "How is it going?" I ask. "We miss you," he says.

■ ■ ■ ■

I have the dog at least. And maybe a little crush too. The guy from the bus came into the library today. He's been wandering in and out of the stacks all morning. Now he's talking to one of the regulars, that woman whose nails look bitten to the quick. "Don't eat plants with milky sap. The exception is dandelions," he tells her. He goes outside to smoke.

By the time I go to lunch, he's nowhere to be seen. I give the woman on the bench her dollar. It's muggy out. I can feel the sweat pooling under my arms. *No one's looking at you,* as my mother used to say.

When I get home, Henry is lying on the couch staring at the ceiling. I find a show that has nothing to do with either of us. We watch, eating huge bowls of chocolate pudding. A contestant faces the camera and talks about her hopes and dreams. Why are people on reality shows always setting their intentions? Is that like prayer for pharmaceutical reps?

■ ■ ■ ■

It feels weird in the building now with Ben gone. Like people are looking differently at me. For example, I can't tell if the drug dealer wants to sleep with me or just with everyone. He gives off sort of an ambient vibe.

He likes me better ever since he saw me

come home the other night at two a.m., stumble drunk. He passed me in the lobby as I tried and retried to use my mailbox key. You good? he asked. I'm good, I said. He went upstairs, but after that he always holds the elevator door for me even when I am halfway across the lobby.

■ ■ ■ ■

It is important to remember that emotional pain comes in waves. Remind yourself that there will be a pause between the waves. That's what Margot told Henry. We've been trying and failing to do the homework.

"It's unbearable," Henry says. "It's barely bearable," she corrects him. He is supposed to record the worst of his visions. "Write it down in first person. Use clear details," she tells him.

Later, I hold Iris while Henry tries to do it. Oh, his eyes — it hurts to look at them. He stumbles, starts over, reads from the beginning.

I leave the baby in the car while I go into the store. It is so much bigger than I expected. I keep wandering up and down the aisles, putting more and more things into my cart. It is so full I even fill up the seat part where the kid is supposed to sit. Suddenly, I remember Iris and run outside. It is a sweltering day and all the windows are closed. There are people standing around the car, trying to break in. A man is hitting the window with a hammer, but it won't break. A woman is screaming. The police come and they smash it open. They give her CPR, but she is already dead. I am standing in the crowd. Then they realize I am her father.

I kiss the baby's head where the soft spot is. "Good," I tell him.

■ ■ ■ ■

That robot Samantha is in the news again. She was on display at a tech conference in Europe. But too many men tried to test her at once, and by the end of the day she was heavily soiled and had two broken fingers.

Her inventor was shaken; he had to ship her back to Spain to be fixed. Luckily, her voice box still worked. I am fine, she said. These people are barbarians, he told a reporter.

Buddhist practice includes the notion that we have all been born many times before and that we have all been each other's mothers and fathers and children and siblings. Therefore, we should treat each person we encounter as if they are our beloved.

■ ■ ■ ■

I've been thinking more about my doom-stead. Choosing people for it is tricky. First, you must assess their character. Will they lead, will they follow? Will they dominate others the moment this becomes possible? Are they alpha? Beta?

My dog, I was told, is neither. She is a climber, which means she will show defer-ence to any alpha dog, but if she has a chance she will creep up farther and farther on the bed until she is found out and pushed down again. The beta would just automatically stay at the foot of the bed.

Second, you must balance the skills of the people you choose. Is one handy? Is one musical? Is one medical?

Third, you must figure out how to tell them you have drafted them for your doomstead.

■ ■ ■ ■

Sometimes I slip up and allow myself for a moment to think of what is wrong with Henry. If he were to get really high and those thoughts came. Then there is the press of strangers against me and I'm up the stairs and into the sunlight again.

■ ■ ■ ■

We watch the season finale of *Extreme Cou-*

poning together. This time the shopper gets her total down to $2.58. Everyone in the store cheers as the train of silver carts is wheeled out to her car.

Earlier in the show, they had given her backstory. This woman wore a dress and lipstick every day to work, but she wasn't afraid to climb into dumpsters to retrieve discarded circulars. The host of the show noted that she'd recently converted her house to storage for bulk buys and now lived with her family in their half-finished basement.

■ ■ ■ ■

My mother sends me a picture. She took a bus with her prayer group to a detention center in the next state. They were not allowed to talk to the people being held there, but they stood outside the barbed wire fence and sang in hopes of cheering them. The picture is of a spindly tree outside the fence. Apparently, it is the only tree visible from the prison. They hung their cross necklaces on its branches before they left.

You are not going to have to walk thirty-four miles with your child on your back.

But if I did.

■ ■ ■ ■

I've been hanging out too much at my old bar while everyone's away. It's fun to talk to people who don't know anything about me. And I spend a lot of time eavesdropping too.

It is important to be on the alert for "the decisive moment," says the man next to me who is talking to his date. I agree. The only difference is that he is talking about twentieth-century photography and I am talking about twenty-first-century every-thing.

Then one day my guy comes in. His name is Will. Turns out he's some kind of journalist. Recently back from Syria. He has an odd side gig: taking kids out for wilderness trips. "No set line between lost and not lost," he tells me, and I write this down on a napkin.

And then somehow, it's four drinks later, and I'm telling him about the coming chaos. "What are you afraid of?" he asks me, and the answer, of course, is dentistry, humiliation, scarcity; then he says, "What are your most useful skills?" "People think I'm funny, I know how to tell a story in a brisk, winning way. I try not to go on much about my discarded ambitions or how I hate hippies and the rich." "But in terms of skills," he says, and I tell him I know a few poems by heart, I recently learned how to make a long-burning candle out of a can of tuna (oil packed, not water), I've learned how to recognize a black walnut tree and that you can live on the inner bark of a birch tree if need be, I know it is important to carry chewing gum at all times for post-collapse morale and also because it suppresses the appetite and you can supposedly fish with it, but only if it is a bright color and has sugar — only then will a fish investigate and somehow get hooked to the end of the fishing pole I have fashioned with a sharpened paper clip and a string and a stick. If you need to, you can use wet tobacco as a poultice over a wound. Red ants can be eaten (they have a lemony taste); the Mormons ate lily bulbs, a famine food; Malcolm X said his mom would make soup out of dandelions when there wasn't enough to eat. If you don't have enough water, don't eat, keep your mouth closed, conserve your energy. You can last three hours without shelter, three days without water, three weeks without food, three months without hope, but don't drink your own urine — that is a myth — and don't eat snow — you have to melt it first. If you have a toothache you can put crushed aspirin on it. All you need to make toothpaste is baking soda, peppermint oil, and water. You can chew on a stick until it splinters into a toothbrush . . .

He keeps touching my arm, this guy. Sometimes your heart runs away with someone and all it takes is a bandanna on a stick.

When I come home, Henry is playing video games. I look at the list of prepper acronyms I printed out this morning.

GOOD = Get Out of Dodge
DTA = Don't Trust Anyone
FUD = Fear, Uncertainty, and Doubt
BSTS = Better Safe Than Sorry
WROL = Without Rule of Law
YOYO = You're on Your Own
INCH = I'm Never Coming Home

■ ■ ■ ■

The next time, I tell him about how soon they will build a seawall around the city. Already, the mayor is getting advice from the Dutch. There are seaside villages in the Netherlands where you can hear waves crashing, see seagulls circling, and smell the salt water without ever once seeing the sea.

He's charismatic, this one, used to being pursued. One night he showed me a picture of his ex-wife, who is a ridiculously hot photojournalist. She's French. He's French Canadian. They used to go to war zones together. I asked him if he'd only ever dated beautiful women. He paused kindly, thought about it. Sort of, he said. Does she have an eye patch? No eye patch, Will said.

Later, after he leaves, Tracy says I'm a loser for not making a move on him. "You should just stay married," she tells me. "I am married," I point out pedantically. "Right," she says.

■ ■ ■ ■

I just . . . I couldn't bear the part where you fell out of love with me, I tell the guy who smiles at me on the subway. Telepathically. But he hears me. Now he's playing some game on his phone, not looking at me at all.

If he runs off with Tracy, I'll be fine. Law of the land. Assortative mating. There's no way I would throw myself in front of a train. Not a chance. But there are always those single-car tree accidents; I could be the other girl in the car. They'd walk away holding hands, but they'll never get over me.

■ ■ ■ ■

One of the things I like about Will is that he doesn't seem to mind if I blather on about zazen. I can tell he's firmly in the school of whatever gets you through the night. I wonder sometimes what he's doing here. "Just passing through," he says. Right, right, ramble on, sing your song, that kind of thing probably.

It takes me a while to piece together what he does with his time. As far as I can tell, he goes somewhere terrible, almost gets killed, then leaves and wanders around some peacetime place until he's ready to go back to reporting again.

He tells me about how he used to go on these long treks. Once he followed the path of an eighteenth-century adventurer. He walked where he walked, stayed where he had stayed. He used the man's journal as a guide. Writing his own book as he went. It became a kind of overlay to the first one, he said. The trip took eight months. There were a few times his feet left the ground. Once on a rainy day, he accepted a ride in a car and was stunned at how violent this new speed felt to his body. His thoughts could not unfold calmly, they were all in a jumble.

He clutched the side of the door and waited in a panic to be released.

How is your walk? That's what they used to ask us at youth group. With Jesus, they meant.

■ ■ ■ ■

My question for Will is: Does this feel like a country at peace or at war? I'm joking, sort of, but he answers seriously.

He says it feels the way it does just before it starts. It's a weird thing, but you learn to pick up on it. Even while everybody's convincing themselves it's going to be okay, it's there in the air somehow. The whole thing is more physical than mental, he tells me.

Like hackles? The way a dog's hackles go up? Yes, he says.

He tells me that at the wilderness camp they

teach the kids something called "loss-proofing." In order to survive, you have to think first of the group. If you look after the needs of others, it will give you purpose and purpose gives you the burst of strength you need in an emergency. He says you never know which kids will do well. But in general the suburban kids do the worst. They have no predators, he says.

■ ■ ■ ■

I don't know how Ben did it. I have to call and get instructions about how to get all the mouse shit off the spice rack and the shelf beneath it, because it's been an hour already with the yellow gloves and the disinfectant and the wet paper towels and so much throwing away of paper that I've already undone all the good I'd done in the world until now. But then I have to put everything back — does that mean I have to wash each spice, each bottle, individually too? "I did," he says sweetly, "but no, I don't think you have to, just getting rid of the shit is great." He laughs when I tell him how long I've been working on it and says, "It's a new day."

I'm starting to miss him. The warm hum of his body next to me in bed. Certain little jokes and kindnesses. A kind of credit or goodwill, extended and extended again and again whether or not you deserve it.

Funny how when you're married all you want is to be anonymous to each other again, but when you're anonymous all you want is to be married and reading together in bed.

■ ■ ■ ■

The email keeps coming. And people have ideas. Don't engineer the sun or the ocean, engineer us.

Smaller people tend to live longer, *one scientist says.* They use less fabric for their clothes, less rubber for their shoes and they fit into airplanes better.

195

Q: What would it mean to bioengineer humans to be more efficient?

A: One thing they looked into were cat eyes, the technique of giving humans cat eyes or of making their eyes more catlike. The reason is that cat eyes see nearly as well as human eyes during the day, but much better at night. The researchers figured that if everyone had cat eyes, you wouldn't need so much lighting, and so you could reduce global energy usage considerably.

I read about all of this in the periodicals room. Other stuff too. There's one journal that's filled with studies about loneliness and how to combat it.

Hunt et al. (1992) found that a woman sitting in a park received significantly more social approaches from passersby whenever she was accompanied by a rabbit or turtle, than when she sat alone with a television set or blowing bubbles.

The adjunct seems paler than usual. He

isn't speaking in complete sentences. Would it be possible to . . . ? Do you mind if . . . ?

They say when you're lonely you start to lose words.

■ ■ ■ ■

Later, in the middle of the night, I start worrying about him. Thinking about things I should have said. I know the things you are supposed to look for. I grew up with the list in my head. Do you have a plan? I'd ask Henry when he called late at night, trying to give away something he no longer needed.

I'd talk and talk, but when he wanted to get off the phone, I'd claim that I had one more thing to say, something I'd forgotten, something important. I need to talk to you in the morning, I'd say. You have to call me back so I can remember. A simple trick, but it worked. Get them to commit to the next day, the next hour, the next minute even.

■ ■ ■ ■

Scientists say that the theory of everything is a technical expression, not a metaphysical one.

But a lot of people who hang out at this bar seem to have grand unifying theories. I heard a lot of them back when I used to bartend here. For a long time, what I picked up on were the grief ones. The way they'd wince if you made a small domestic complaint; the way they radiated anger at your belief the ground was solid beneath your feet.

Lately, I've been noticing the sex ones, the people who've been all the way down the line and back again. They know every way a person can be broken or break; they know how to be the hammer and the nail. "Can I ask you something?" Will says and I say "Sure, ask me something."

"How do you know all this?"
"I'm a fucking librarian."

■ ■ ■ ■

People Also Ask

What will disappear from stores first?
Why do humans need myths?
Do we live in the Anthropocene?
What is the cultural trance?
Is it wrong to eat meat?
What is surveillance capitalism?
How can we save the bees?
What is the internet of things?
When will humans go extinct?

■ ■ ■ ■

Sylvia decides to stop recording interviews.
She tells me to go through the archive and
pick which ones to air.

I played the one by that disaster psychologist again. He explains that in times of
emergency the brain can get stuck on a

loop, trying to find a similar situation for comparison.

This is why you must make a plan before disaster strikes. In a hotel, study the fire exits. On a ferry, look for the life jackets. On a plane, read the card they tell you to read.

Without such a plan, people quickly lose their bearings. Husbands leave behind their wives. Parents flee without their children. You might even repeat to yourself, like a mantra, *I have children! I have children!*

■ ■ ■ ■

One weekend my brother and I house-sit for Sylvia. I'm edgy, restless, thinking of things I shouldn't be. There are so many mice in the walls it is impossible to sleep. They make that noise that is somewhere between a skittering and a whirring. And some animal gnawed through the protective casing on the propane tank. Henry's eyes look bad. This morning we got up very early to look at a rare and particular kind of moon.

And I need to get my mother's teeth fixed. A wisdom one's infected, another is crumbling. She told me her plan is to drive to the clinic at the university four hours away. People come from much farther, from miles and miles away, so many that when you get there, there is a lottery system to see who gets to have their pain taken away. America is the name of this place where you can win big.

■ ■ ■ ■

Do you want to hang out in the daylight? Will texts me when I get back. I wait until my brother has a friend over and then I go out for a cheat walk with him. We go to a little park I've never been to before. Maybe it's near where he lives. We never talk about where we live.

There's a little pond in the middle of it. We wonder how deep it is. I find a stick, hand it

201

to him. "Women are equal now," he says, but he throws it just to humor me.

Prepper tip: If you are caught without any gear, all you need to fish is some spit and your shirt. Wade out into the water, then lift up your shirt to make a net beneath the water's surface. Spit as much as you can into it. Minnows will be attracted to it because they think it's food. When you have several of them investigating, jerk your shirt up out of the water. Now you have dinner.

Will laughs when I tell him this. "There are better ways," he says. "I grew up fishing." He grew up out in the middle of nowhere, snow up to their windows.

So sure, maybe I could charm him for a while, but when the shine wore off? How long until he figured out I can't chop wood or light a fire? Ben is used to my all talk, no action ways, but it took a long time to bank all that goodwill.

The thought of having to be with someone

else long enough to deserve it again. That's what feels impossible. Because the part where they are charmed by you, where you are every good thing, and then the part later — sooner, maybe, but always later — where they tire of you, of all your repetitions, of all your little and big shames, I don't think I could bear that. Tracy says nonsense, I should seize the moment, have a fling while Ben's away. And I could, right? I could! I could!

All I would have to do is take my clothes off with a stranger who has no particular interest in my long-term well-being or mental stability. How hard is that? I could do that. It would be fun. Especially if said stranger got all my jokes, and liked how I never nagged and how I never asked if I looked fat, and would agree to make me go to the dentist and doctor even though I don't ever want to (because of death, death, the terrible death), and would be okay with my indifferent housekeeping and my seventies-style bush, and would be okay with us having to take care of my brother financially and emotionally for the rest of his life, also my mother, who is good and kind, but doesn't have a cent, then I'm totally into it,

I'd happily fuck him whichever way he fancied until the bright morn.

But also I'm married. Happily, I'd say. So what we do mostly is we text each other. The moment we part. Stupid things, little jokes about the news or our days. Sometimes I send them late at night, but when I do they are scrupulously chaste. This tonight from the bathroom: *kompromat on me: electric toothbrush now manual.*

■ ■ ■ ■

Sometimes Will flinches when I stray off the paved sidewalk onto the grass. He's got lots of good stories. None of them are about war.

Well, that's not true. That one time he talked about war, or not quite about war, but about the time just before it. He said your body knew things before your brain did. You started noticing different things.

Are you sure you're not a spy? Because you

204

kind of seem like a spy, I told him once. I'm not a spy, he said. But I could send you a message in code.

■ ■ ■ ■

In class, a woman talks about what has happened to her. She has some kind of illness where the lightest of touches is painful to the skin. "I can't bear it," she says. Margot nods. You can barely bear it, I think reflexively.

There are different stories about how Margot's husband died. He was stung by a bee, I think. Somehow he never had been before in all his life and he was deathly allergic.

In some Zen monasteries, gossip is defined as talking about anything not directly in one's gaze.

■ ■ ■ ■

Henry's box is full of scraps of paper,

phrases in micro-script. We both have dreams about people finding it. In the beginning, it took a week to fill. But this time just four days. Often these thoughts get worse before they get better, Margot said. This is to be expected. But you can expect something and still get the breath knocked out of you by it.

"Shall we start?" I ask him. Henry nods, hunches his shoulders. The park is mostly empty because it's cold. We're on an out of the way bench. As instructed, he reads each one aloud to me. The baby is burned, smothered, strangled, flayed. I rip them into pieces, throw them away.

Later, I ride the elevator up with the drug dealer from 5C. How about this mother-fucking darkness? is what our eyes say.

■ ■ ■ ■

I decide to ask Will if he's ever been to a shrink. "Nothing happened to me," he says. He waves his hand in a general way that seems to mean, Look, one piece, not blown to bits. "Right," I say. "Gotcha." Lots going on in that harrowed head of his, I bet. There is a weird pause and then he shifts into another topic in that gear-stripping way of his.

"How was your walk with Henry?" he says. "Nothing happened to me either," I tell him.

∎ ∎ ∎ ∎

Okay, okay, turn off the light. Go to sleep. I have Ambien, but I want the other drugs, the gladdening drugs. I take it but somehow still wake up at three a.m.

Where is my husband? Where is my son?

We've never talked about Eli. Just once he asked me if he knew how to hunt or fish. I laughed because of where we live. But that night, in bed, I thought, Oh, Canada!

Because I can't seem to escape that question. What will be the safest place? There was that climatologist on television the other night. She was talking about her own children.

I find it really hard to decide on one particular region, saying this one is going to be safe and we are just going to lock this one in. I don't think there will be any safe places. I am . . . the impacts are going to be big. So my approach is to be as mobile, as flexible as possible, to be able to adapt to whatever is going to happen. My children are bilingual and we're working on a third language. Both children have three passports, and they actually have the freedom to be able to study and work even in the European Union, or in Canada, or in Australia.

■ ■ ■ ■

My mother calls to tell me she is buying socks in bulk and handing them out to all the homeless people she sees. And she tries to keep a stack of dollar bills in the glove compartment so she can give at least one with each pair of socks. My mother who lives on a tiny fixed income. She's putting too much wear and tear on the car, I worry. It has so many miles on it already.

A brother questioned a Desert Father about his life. And he said:

> Eat straw, wear straw, sleep on straw: that is to say, despise everything and acquire for yourself a heart of iron.

There have been a few signs that Catherine's tilting into the abyss too. Lately, she's been forwarding me these weird emails.

> <u>Please share!</u>
> Parents and children were really one in the beginning and grew as a kind of plant. But then they separated and became two, and begat children. And they loved the children so much that they ate them up. God thought, "Well, this can't go on." So he reduced parental love by something like ninety-nine and nine-tenths percent, so parents wouldn't eat up their children.

I've printed it out to show Henry. But he doesn't laugh. "She's a good person," he says. "So are you," I say.

Then just as I'm remembering that we are all one people, that we all have hopes and dreams, I see Mrs. Kovinski coming down the street toward me. We avoid each other now. Ever since I told her I would not listen to her hate.

■ ■ ■ ■

I've been telling Will about the cards I help Henry write. "I want a card!" he says. So I write him one on a napkin.

Roses are red,
Violets are blue,
I feel slightly less dread,
When I am with you.

He's going back home soon. He wants to live near the woods again. Somewhere in Quebec.

The other night he gave me a book: *Code of Maritime Signals,* 1931 edition. Beside some of them were tiny pencil dots.

"I wish to communicate with you."
"Stop carrying out your intentions and watch for my signals."
"I am on fire."
"Nothing can be done until the weather moderates."

■ ■ ■ ■

On his last day, we go to the aquarium. My favorite are the manta rays. We watch them wing past. They have the largest brain of any fish, I remember. If you put them in front of a mirror, they do not behave as if they see another ray. Instead they glide and watch, dip and wave.

"What's keeping you here?" he says. Please, I think, but no, I can't even look at him. All these people. I have so many people, you wouldn't believe it.

Five

A man is having terrible dreams. In them, he is being chased by a demon. He seeks counsel from a therapist, who tells him he must turn around and confront the demon or he will never escape it. He vows to do this, but each night in his dreams, he runs again. Finally, he manages to turn around and look straight at the demon. "Why are you chasing me?" he asks it. The demon says, "I don't know. It's your dream."

After he left, I realized he had inscribed the book for me. I wondered how he'd sign it. There are all those ways to be careful: *yrs* or *warmly* or *best.* He's clever though. *MY-BAS.* Even if Ben saw it, he wouldn't guess. A prepper joke.

May You Be Among the Survivors.

It's cold turkey, this thing sometimes. I'm sweating it out. Music helps a bit.

Can I kick it?

Yes, you can.

■ ■ ■ ■

I try to explain to Tracy about Will. How it was like a wartime romance. Minus the war. Minus the sex. She looks at me. "So nothing happened?" she says.

And then it is another day and another and another, but I will not go on about this because no doubt you too have experienced time.

Q: How do you maintain your optimism?

A: If you are not getting enough iron, put a few iron nails into a bowl of lemon juice and leave it overnight. In the morning, make lemonade out of it.

Mom? Mom? Mom?

∎ ∎ ∎ ∎

Little flickers sometimes, things I want to tell him. At the bodega, I buy a cucumber from Mohan.

You can obtain plants more easily and more quietly than meat. This is extremely important when the enemy is near.

Then one day I have to run to catch a bus. I am so out of breath when I get there that I know in a flash all my preparations for the apocalypse are doomed. I will die early and ignobly.

∎ ∎ ∎ ∎

"There are ancient ways of prepping too," Ben says. The mystery cultists believed that the first thing a newly dead soul would see in the underworld was the spring of Lethe. It would be found flowing beneath a white cypress tree. The soul would arrive very thirsty but must resist the temptation to drink, because the waters of this spring were the waters of oblivion. Part of the training of the mystery cultists was to learn to endure extreme thirst.

Consider the earth's diminished radiance . . .

I remember on our first date, I waited for Ben to tell me about his awful childhood or his newly acquired drug habit, etc., etc., but instead, he told me about the community garden he was involved in. He was having trouble with the eggplant, he said. He had hopes for it though. Maybe if there was a little more rain or a little more sun. I can't remember now which one he needed.

■ ■ ■ ■

There was once a Desert Father who was able to banish demons, and he asked them

afterward,
What makes you go away? Is it fasting?
We do not eat or drink, they replied.
Is it vigils?
We do not sleep, they replied.
Is it separation from the world?
We live in the deserts.
What power sends you away then?
Nothing can overcome us except humility,
they told him.

■ ■ ■ ■

They are playing a board game when I come
home. "If you give me wood, I'll give you
some wheat and a brick," Eli says to Ben.

I asked her once what I could do, how I
could get him ready. It would be good if he
had some skills, she said. And of course, no
children.

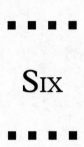

SIX

I go to get my permanent crown. I have been putting off my dental work, but now I go. The hygienist talks to me about the weather. The dentist comes in with his gloved hands and mask. He says I have an unusually small mouth. I open it wider for him.

∎ ∎ ∎ ∎

There was once a race of mythic arctic dwellers called the Hyperboreans. Their weather was mild, their trees bore fruit all year, and no one was ever sick. But after a thousand years, they grew bored of this life. They decked themselves in garlands and leaped off the cliffs into the sea.

"What is the core delusion?" Margot asks the class, but nobody knows the right answer, and she doesn't bother to tell us.

■ ■ ■ ■

As soon as he got back, Ben made me make an appointment to get this mole on my arm checked. I stood there in my dingy bra and Target underwear while the doctor examined me. He was well groomed with a plume of silver-gray hair and an unplaceable European accent. He held a magnifying glass up to my skin. Described every mark on my body one by one: Exceedingly unlikely to be cancerous! Exceedingly unlikely to be cancerous!

He had a melodious voice. I wanted every day to be like this, to begin in shame and fear and end in glorious reassurance.

■ ■ ■ ■

Do not believe that because you are a revolutionary you must feel sad.

■ ■ ■ ■

Ben and I made a list of requirements for our doomstead: arable land, a water source, access to a train line, high on a hill. Are we on a hill for floods or defense? Both. I'll build a moat, he said, then went on the internet to learn how to do it.

You must own small, unnoticeable items. For example, a generator is good, but 1,000 BIC lighters are better. A generator will attract attention if there's any trouble, but 1,000 lighters are compact, cheap, and can always be traded.

"Wait, when did you take up smoking?" Ben says when he finds them in a drawer.

Something happened while he was away. He did the math, all the math, and now there's a quote from Epictetus pinned above his desk.

You are not some disinterested bystander/ Exert yourself.

■ ■ ■ ■

In those disaster movies, the hero always says, "Trust me," and the one who is about to die says, "Do I have a choice?"

"No."

That's what the hero says.

■ ■ ■ ■

I take Eli to the playground. Someone walks past with his head down, swiping right, swiping left. The buildings look whitewashed in light. The air smells sweet. Diminishing radiance, but still some, I'd say.

I've changed my mind. You can have a child. It will be small and cat-eyed. It will never know the taste of meat.

Q: What is the difference between a disaster and an emergency?

A: A disaster is a sudden event that causes great damage or loss. An emergency is a situation in which normal operations cannot continue and immediate action is required so as to prevent a disaster.

What if we went for a walk, if we walked out into the streets?

It's impossible.
It's barely possible.

■ ■ ■ ■

Sri Ramakrishna said, *Do not seek illumination unless you seek it as a man whose hair is on fire seeks a pond.*

■ ■ ■ ■

It still comes back to me sometimes, the way the light came through those windows. The dust had a presence. At least if you stared at it long enough, it did.

The Unitarians never kneel. But I want to kneel. Later, I do at home by my bed. The oldest and best of prayers: *Mercy.*

■ ■ ■ ■

I go to church with my mother. I pray fumblingly for strength, for grace. Sunlight pours through the windows. There's that dust I remember. Soon it will be time to shake hands with those around me and speak to them. But I don't know what is in their hearts. One of you will betray me, I think. But my mother is so happy I have come. She sits as close to me as she can. The minister speaks of the invisible and visible worlds, but not of how to tell the difference. An old white man in the next pew is the first to turn and reach for my hand.

Peace be with you.
And also with you.

■ ■ ■ ■

Sylvia calls me. All that sky makes her more patient now when I talk about the mystics.

There's that idea in the different traditions. Of the veil. What if we were to tear through it? (Welcome, say the ferns. We've been expecting you.)

"Of course, the world continues to end," Sylvia says, then gets off the phone to water her garden.

■ ■ ■ ■

If you think you are lost: beware bending the map. Don't say maybe it was a pond, not a lake; maybe the stream flowed east, not west. Leave a trail as you go. Try to mark trees.

Paper ballots, paper ballots, everyone said, but I put the final card in a machine. There's a bunch of us now milling around outside the building. Put your hackles up, I think.

Hello? Hello?
What is —
What is your emergency?

They say people who are lost will walk trancelike past their own search parties. Maybe I saw you. Maybe I passed you on my street. How will I know you? Trust me, you'll say.

■ ■ ■ ■

On the way home, the wind blows some newspapers down the street. There's a man sleeping in a doorway and one comes and curls itself around his feet.

A visitor asked the old monks at Mount Athos what they did all day and was told: *We have died and we are in love with everything.*

■ ■ ■ ■

We don't know if it's a new mouse or the old mouse. This is the fatal flaw of the have-a-heart trap, Ben's sister says. Some use paint to mark each one. Fool me once, etc., etc. But they have not gotten to that point yet. When we house-sit for them, it falls to Ben to do the work. First with the neck breaking and then with the releasing. Three nights in a row now. We hear the mouse in the trap rattling. Ben gets out of bed, puts on his shoes, permits himself a sigh. I pull the covers up while he puts the trap on the passenger seat and then drives a mile down the dirt road to the big field. But the drive is awkward. Captor, captive. The moonlight through the windshield. No one talks, he says.

At night, the floorboards creak. Henry is pacing back and forth upstairs. He is trying to wear himself out or maybe he is trying to wear Iris out. Either is fine because nobody's crying. He's got his six-month sobriety chip now. He's had these chips before, but he keeps this one in his wallet at least. In the past, he's just let Eli play bodega with them.

The dentist gave me something so I won't grind my teeth in my sleep. I consider putting it in, decide against it. My husband is under the covers reading a long book about an ancient war. He turns out the light, arranges the blankets so we'll stay warm. The dog twitches her paws softly against the bed. Dreams of running, of other animals. I wake to the sound of gunshots. Walnuts on the roof, Ben says. The core delusion is that I am here and you are there.

www.obligatorynoteofhope.com

ACKNOWLEDGMENTS

I want to thank the John Simon Memorial Foundation for their generous support of my work.

I could not have finished this book without the gift of time and space granted to me by the Macdowell Colony and by Art Omi.

Thank you to the Abramovich Foundation, the Beckman House, the Blaine Colony, the Kearney Farm, and the Koehlert Cottage for offering me impromptu residencies when I most needed them.

Thank you to my parents, David and Jane Offill, for moral and logistical support when I was wild-eyed with deadline anxiety.

Thank you to my editor, Jordan Pavlin, and to my agent, Sally Wofford-Girand, who gave me brilliant advice and patient encouragement along the way.

Thank you to Laura Barber and all the excellent folks at *Granta* for their help.

Thank you to Tasha Blaine and Joshua Beckman for showing me the way through the earliest drafts.

Thank you Alex Abramovich, Dawn Breeze, Taylor Curtin, Jonathan Dee, Eugenia Dubini, Lamorna Elmer, Rachel Fershleiser, Rebecca Godfrey, Hallie Goodman, Jackie Goss, Maggie Goudsmit, Gioia Guerzoni, Irene Haslund, J. Haynes, Amy Hufnagel, Samantha Hunt, Brennan Kearney, Fred Leebron, Ben Lerner, Kyo Maclear, Rita Madrigal, Lydia Millet, Emily Reardon, Elissa Schappell, Rob Spillman, Dana Spiota, Kieran Suckling, Nicholas Thomson, Eirik Solheim, and Jennifer Wai-lam Strodl.

And most of all, for everything, thanks to Dave and Theodora and Jetta the dog.

NOTES

58 "Breathing in, I know that I am of the nature to": This is a from a traditional Buddhist chant called "The Five Remembrances." The meditation teacher has very loosely adapted it and is only doing four of the five. The original can be found in *Plum Village Chanting and Recitation Book* as compiled by Thich Nhat Hanh and the Monks and Nuns of Plum Village.

75 "One night a house": Prose poem told by Inugpasugjuk. *Technicians of the Sacred,* ed. Jerome Rothernburg. Garden City, NY: Anchor Books, 1969.

108 "by persons who are acquainted with the science": I am indebted to Clive Hamilton, who retells this story in "Why We Resist the Truth About Climate Change," which was given as a paper at the Science and Politics conference held at the Museum of Natural Sciences in Brussels, October 28, 2010. The original story is

found in *Arms and the Covenant: Speeches by the Right Hon. Winston Churchill,* George C. Harrap & Ltd, 1938. The speech referenced was given to the Commons on July 30, 1934.

122 "The critical question for our generation": This quotation is from *God Is the Gospel: Meditations on God's Love as the Gift of Himself* by John Piper.

125 "Trace the water you drink": This is adapted from "Where You At? A Bioregional Quiz," developed by Leonard Charles, Jim Dodge, Lynn Milliman, and Victoria Stockley, which was published in *Coevolution Quarterly* 32 (Winter 1981).

196 "Hunt et al. (1992) found that a woman": This is excerpted from the article "The Value of Pets for Human Health" in the March 2011 issue of *The Psychologist.*

208 "I find it really hard to decide on one particular region": The speaker here is Professor Katrin Meissner, Director, UNSW, Climate Change Research Centre. She is quoted in a transcript of the show *ABC Lateline,* hosted by Kerry Brewster, entitled "Climate Scientists Reveal Their Fears for the Future." The transcript is dated June 27, 2017.

ABOUT THE AUTHOR

Jenny Offill is the author of the novels *Last Things* (a *New York Times* Notable Book and a finalist for the L.A. Times First Fiction Award) and *Dept. of Speculation,* which was short-listed for the Folio Prize, the PEN/Faulkner Award, and the International Dublin Literary Award. She lives in upstate New York and teaches at Syracuse University and in the low-residency MFA program at Queens University.